A gigantic dam is to be built at Veere, Holland, closing off the sea forever longer will the small village be a tling town of fishermen and their families, no longer will the ships sail in and out of the harbor. For twelve-year-old Machiel Cevaal and his friends, a way of life is about to end. And at the same time, Machiel must plan for his future— should he become a fisherman like his father and brother, or should he become an engineer and work on dams like the one at Veere?

The way in which Machiel handles this conflict and others is a vital part of this modern Dutch novel, a story that will absorb and delight young American readers.

GERTIE EVENHUIS lived for ten years in the Zeeland region of Holland, which is the setting for *Locked Harbor*. She is the author of eight books for children, and now makes her home in Amsterdam.

LOCKED HARBOR

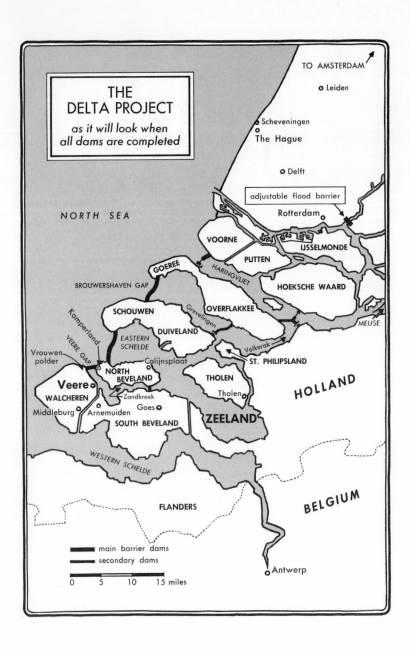

GERTIE EVENHUIS

LOCKED
HARBOR

Translated by EVA RICHTER

THE MACMILLAN COMPANY, NEW YORK
COLLIER-MACMILLAN LIMITED, LONDON

For Michaël—Marnix

Originally published in Dutch as *Verdreven Vloot*
in 1962 by Uitgeverij Ploegsma, Amsterdam, the Netherlands
Copyright © The Macmillan Company 1967
Map and drawing by Phero Thomas
The Macmillan Company, New York
Collier-Macmillan Canada, Ltd., Toronto, Ontario
Library of Congress catalog card number: 67-21246
Printed in the United States of America
First Printing

Contents

THE CAISSONS

AUTHOR'S NOTE

For centuries Holland has been building and maintaining its dikes with great vigilance. This small country has had no choice: much of its land consists of polders, which lie below sea level, and much has been reclaimed from the sea. And for centuries it has been necessary to build dikes to enclose miles and miles of the enormously long coast lines which face not only the North Sea, but also the large inland seaways.

Despite careful maintenance of its dikes, Holland has often suffered from the ravages of water, and in 1953 an immensely powerful storm flooded the land and killed eight hundred people; thousands had to flee their homes. It was the country's worst flood since 1421. Particularly hard hit was the Zeeland area, Southwest Holland, which is the setting for this story. Although measures for better protection of the land against the sea were already being studied, immediately after the 1953 disaster the Government set up a group called the Delta Commission to suggest bold new plans for safeguarding the country in the future. (The name Delta was chosen because three rivers—the Rhine, the Schelde and the Meuse—form a delta where they flow out of Holland into the North Sea.) The Delta Project, the result of the Commission's study, called for enormous dams to close off four of the large sea inlets, the Haringvliet, the Brouwershaven Gap, the Eastern Schelde and the Veere Gap. In addition, secondary dams have been built in the Zandkreek, Grevelingen and Volkerak.

The dam which closed the Veere Gap and the secondary dam in the Zandkreek are together referred to as the Three-Island Project, because they connect the islands of Walcheren, North Beveland and South Beveland.

Two major inlets, the Rotterdam Waterway and the Western Schelde, both of which are vital to Holland's commercial activity, will remain open to provide continued access to the ports of Rotterdam and Antwerp.

When the gigantic new dams are closed, and the sea blocked off, the water in the inland waterways will be converted to fresh water. The waterways will become lakes, and will be used for recreation activities such as swimming and sailing. The country will be protected not only against flooding but also against the salt which had been seeping into the land and endangering farm crops.

The dams being built as part of the Delta Project differ from one another in size and design. The center section of the dam at Veere is made up of watertight caissons, enormous concrete boxes with doors which can be moved vertically. The caissons are built on land, and, at the proper time, floated out and placed into position. Precise calculations are then made to determine when the portcullises should be let down, permanently sealing off the sea. Others have sluice gates so that the ice which comes down the rivers in wintertime and fishing boats and other shipping can be let out into the sea.

I have already referred to the huge size of these dams, and they are, in fact, so large that highways (in some cases with six lanes) are being built upon them, connecting parts of Holland which have been isolated by the sea for centuries. Although the Netherlands is a small country, communication between some areas—Walcheren and North Beveland, for example—has been difficult and time-consuming because of inadequate road and ferry systems.

The entire Delta Project will be completed in 1978, but the closing of the Veere Gap, as described in this story, took place in 1961. For Holland as a nation, the Delta Project is without question a tremendous achievement, essential for the country's future safety, but for those people who are directly affected, it often causes deep and far-reaching changes in their lives. It is about such people that I have written *Locked Harbor,* a story based on the facts discussed in this note.

GERTIE EVENHUIS

LOCKED HARBOR

1
BENEATH THE
CAMPVEERSE TOWER

THE afternoon sun shone on the luminous, gray sea as the five children sat on the wall beneath the Campveerse Tower. The tones of the Town Hall tower carillon striking three-thirty carried over to them on the wind, and the sea gulls screamed and swooped overhead. But otherwise, on the pier, on the fishing wharf and farther to the left where the tall, narrow houses stood, there was no sound. The harbor of Veere was deserted; all the ships were at sea, and only a little life-boat remained, its orange and blue bow barely visible.

The children sat there just as generations of children had sat before them. Machiel Cevaal had a real fisherman's cap on, though it was much too large for him. From beneath the visor he stared sharply and steadily at the point where the Veere Gap gave way to the North Sea. He wanted to be the first to sight the ships, due over the horizon at any moment.

The others talked a bit, swung their wooden shoes against

the wall beneath them and occasionally glanced at the landing stage to their right. But they were watching for the ships too.

Andries Domisse, Machiel's cousin, cocked his head and carefully balanced his swinging wooden shoes on his upturned toes as he looked at the lifeboat.

"Low tide," he remarked. "He ought to watch out for that sand bar."

"And your father ought to watch out for the pier," said Wolfert van Borssele harshly. Andries's father, Skipper Domisse, always cut the sharpest corner possible in coming in, and every day the children secretly hoped he would run into the pier just across from them. But so far the *Ve 13* had escaped without a scratch, and so Andries held his tongue.

"Some day he's going to get smashed," Wolfert forecast.

Wolfert's sister Tannie laughed and said, "Don't let him get your goat, Andries."

Tannie slipped off the wide wall onto the platform built around the Campveerse Tower on the seaside. It served as a pier for the ferryboat to Kamperland. There were crayfish in iron traps hanging in the water. Tannie sat on her heels and moved a trap chain with her fingers until an enormous crayfish rose up, waving its claws.

"It's a shame," she muttered pityingly. "Tomorrow the poor things will probably be lining the stomach of some tourist."

"That's what crayfish are for. And it's a good thing Arjaan catches them, because if they get into a net they tear the whole thing apart and we're left with the holes," said Andries.

"Work's good for you," Wolfert snapped. Andries made a face, and Wolfert began to smile. He knew that Andries hated to mend nets. Then Wolfert jumped off the wall and said, "It's so silly for us to sit here like this every afternoon."

"What's so silly about it?" Andries challenged.

"Just is. The boats will come in whether we're here to watch them or not."

Machiel pulled his cap down over his eyebrows. There was only stony silence from the others.

"We've seen it so often," Wolfert went on. "You won't catch me sitting near the fields all day to see if my father's tractor comes in!" He laughed loudly.

"We didn't drag you here," said Machiel. Then he realized that he couldn't explain why they came to the pier every afternoon to watch for the boats, or why he never got bored with the sea even if there were no boats to look at.

"Always the water," Wolfert grumbled. "And that noise— it's a nuisance."

"But you keep coming back," Tannie pointed out.

"All right!" snapped Wolfert. "*You* tell me what the difference is, Captain Cevaal!" He was sick of Machiel and Andries and their constant talk of the sea, and the ships, and the sand bars, and . . . As though his family's farm on Duchess Hedwina polder wasn't important. "You know, smarty, there are more farmers than fishermen around here!"

A funny look came into Machiel's eyes at Wolfert's contemptuous tone, and it made Wolfert hesitate to say more. Machiel pulled his cap down by the visor and said slowly, "Waiting for the ships is different from sitting around on a farm and waiting for a tractor. If you can't see why, I can't explain it to you."

Tannie could see that the two boys were about to start fighting. "Oh, come on now. Forget it," she said soothingly. "Tractors can be very beautiful," she added, glancing at Wolfert. She couldn't risk riling him too much or he'd get even with her at home when the others weren't there. It wouldn't be the first time.

"Lousy boats," Wolfert muttered. "You wait! Your old shrimp cutters won't be around much longer. My father says . . ."

"Hey! Who's that over there?" Andries suddenly interrupted.

Everyone turned around to look. A strange boy was walking across the jetty ahead of them. His hands were in the pockets of his pea jacket, and he was looking down. Every now and then he would shove a crayfish into the water with his foot. They fell into the water with a little plop.

The boy strolled to the edge of the pier. He took one hand out of his pocket to shade his face as he stared into the distance.

"He's waiting for the ships too," Tannie whispered.

"Yes, but who is he?" Andries hissed.

Tannie giggled. "You can't expect every stranger to ask our permission . . ."

"But this one isn't a tourist," Machiel interrupted. "Those people walk quite differently. This guy's just an ordinary kid."

"But we don't *know* him," said Andries.

Wolfert nodded in agreement. "Yeah! What is *he* doing here?"

The boy stood still, his back turned toward them. The wind blew his dark hair back and forth.

"What's he *doing* here?" Wolfert insisted. "He's walking as though he lived here!" he added, spoiling for a fight.

"With your majesty's permission!" Tannie exclaimed. Wolfert whirled around and swung at her arm. At the same moment the stranger turned toward them, and they suddenly fell silent as he scrutinized their group. They stared back at his narrow face beneath thick, black hair. The stranger turned toward the sea again and then, without hurrying, strolled back across the pier.

"How about that!" Wolfert exclaimed excitedly. "Old stuck-up! Look at him walk!"

"He's just walking," Machiel said calmly. He looked at Andries, who was whistling under his breath and scratching his head as if he was trying to remember something.

"I know!" Andries cried suddenly. "He's one of those people from the Waterworks Authority!"

"Who?" asked Tannie.

"From the Waterworks Authority!" Andries repeated excitedly. "I had to go to the harbor works with Jacob the other day—you know—over where all those strangers are, working on the cranes and the barges. Well, their families have come now, and they're planning to live here. I'll bet he's one of them!"

The fact that the boy was a stranger was something they knew they shouldn't hold against him. But if he was connected with the Waterworks Authority, that was something else again.

"His father must be working on the dam," exclaimed Wolfert. "He's an engineer or something!"

"How would *you* know!" Andries said impatiently.

"My father told me," Wolfert answered heatedly. "They get the ordinary workmen from Zeeland, but the higher-ups are all from Northern Holland. And now their wives and children have come."

Joris Hollebrandse, who had not said a word all afternoon, finally spoke up: "If that's true, they won't be leaving right away. This is going to get bad."

They looked at the great stretch of sea before them; it was known as the Veere Gap, named after their small town on the island of Walcheren. Across the Gap, to their east, was the island of North Beveland, and to the north, of course, was the North Sea, which they could see stretching out endlessly.

Not so long ago, the Veere Gap had been two miles wide. But the previous winter, at Kamperland on the North Beveland side, a massive chunk of dike had been built into the Gap. Half a year later the same thing had been done on the Walcheren side at a spot outside Veere called the Vrouwen polder. Even though the pieces of dike lay a couple of miles from Veere, they could be seen from the Campveerse Tower, and it looked as though a snake without a mid-section was creeping from the Vrouwen polder to Kamperland.

A large gap was still open between the pieces of dike, and the Veere fishermen's ships appeared there against the horizon every afternoon. From their ships the men saw the pieces of dike to the left and right, threatening their way of life. The ships still came in each afternoon and went out each night as they always had, but for three years there had been ominous talk of the great Delta Dam to be built across the inlet, shutting the fishermen off from the sea forever.

Everyone knew that the dam across the Veere Gap was only one of several to be built by the government. Not only would there be this immense dam between the islands of Walcheren and North Beveland, but there would also be dams between North Beveland and Schouwen, between Schouwen and Goeree and between Goeree and Voorne. All these dams were part of an over-all plan called the Delta Project named after the delta formed by the Rhine, the Meuse and the Schelde rivers as they flow into the North Sea. Although the Veere fishermen were vaguely aware of the extent of the plan, they were mainly concerned about the part that would affect them directly, the closing of the Veere Gap. They all knew about it, but they refused to believe it would happen. The fishermen didn't talk about it very much, and when they did they always said, "It won't come to that!" Without saying much more, they simply kept on sailing in and out.

Old Arjaan, who manned the lifeboat, had forecast grimly: "You'll see, whatever the Waterworks people get into their heads comes true sooner or later."

Some fishermen, like Andries's father, Skipper Domisse, had replied heatedly, "But we're still here! Those plans of theirs won't come off so easily!"

Others, like Machiel's father, Skipper Cevaal, had been silent. They still sailed in and out, but their faces were strained whenever they passed the pieces of dike which crept farther and farther into the sea.

And it *had* come to that. The Waterworks Authority people had returned to the North Beveland shore, and from the quay in Veere you could clearly see the wooden sheds near the site, right ahead of Restless Flats, and the cranes with their long, black arms dumping mud by the ton into the splashing water.

There was only three hundred yards open now between the two parts of the dam, and on both sides the cranes, pumps, dredges, flat-bottomed boats, concrete mixers and pile drivers, the scoops and the hurrying tugboats, swarmed unceasingly. The tourists who came to visit the picturesque town saw what was happening, and said that in a year Veere would be a different place. What is left of a harbor town when the ships no longer come in, when the quay remains silent day and night, and when even the sea gulls move farther seaward?

"That kid ought to be ashamed of himself," Tannie said suddenly, breaking the silence.

Machiel burst out laughing. Wasn't that just like Tannie to get so riled, he thought. But she was a good friend, anyway, much better than her troublesome brother Wolfert.

"Well, he should," Tannie insisted. "Mrs. Hubregse said so herself when I went over there this morning with the milk."

"That that guy ought to be ashamed of himself?" Machiel asked, laughing even harder.

"That it was a shame!" Tannie was furious now. " 'All those strange people! They ought to be ashamed of themselves.' That's what she said. 'Building a dam and sticking Veere behind it! And chasing all the fishermen out to Colijnsplaat!' "

"That boy can't very well help it if the dam is being built here," said Machiel. He was still thinking of the other boy's face. He had found it rather pleasant.

"No, but his father can!" Wolfert snapped. It was not often that he agreed with his sister, but he had no use at all for strangers. "The hydraulic engineers are here to work on the caissons. I know, my father told me."

Andries Domisse sniffed scornfully. "What does your father know about it?"

"He's on the Town Council," Wolfert said proudly, but Andries was not impressed. Wolfert! he thought. Always showing off, as if anyone would tell him what had been discussed in the Council.

"Anyway," Wolfert went on, "there's a whole gang of strangers from the North out there, and you can see that they don't intend to leave even a tiny hole in the dike open. Nothing, absolutely nothing."

"What are hydraulic engineers, anyway?" asked Joris.

"They're—oh, you know . . ." Wolfert answered vaguely.

He had to give some answer, as Machiel was looking at him mockingly.

"They're—uh—some of those Delta people," he finished lamely.

"Maybe the fellow who thought up the whole Delta Plan is out there, too," Tannie sulked.

Suddenly a boy's shrill voice sounded behind them: "They're coming!" Wolfert whirled around and ran off with Joris panting behind him.

"Oh, nuts! It's Sjakie!" said Machiel. He had missed being the first to see the ships after all, and all because of that dam. The dam had made his father more silent than ever these past few months; it had made the face of his brother Dingenis harsh, and he hardly ever joked or teased any more; it was making Moei Katrina, his old aunt, try harder than ever to talk him out of becoming a fisherman. And that boy just now . . . So he was one of "those people." He didn't look so bad, but he was just another reminder of all the annoying things that had come up recently. If he hadn't been walking here they wouldn't have got into all that fuss. Machiel was grumpy and ignored Tannie when she asked him to lift her up onto the wall. Sighing, she climbed up herself.

Like black dots the shrimp boats of Veere and Tholen and Arnemuiden were coming in, their nets spread sideways from their masts. It was a sight to watch. Tannie looked at Machiel. The way he sat there, his sharp, dark profile against the blue sky, he looked more like a real fisherman than any of the others. Even his eyes were the color of the sea. But just imagine what would happen if she said anything like that out loud! She blushed at the very thought. But it would be nice to have a brother like him. With his father's cap Machiel looked almost like a man, she thought. Yes, he was a bit stiff, and at times there was something in his face that made one almost afraid—something dark and somber. Machiel's mother had died in the great flood, seven years ago. He did have Moei Katrina to take care of him, but an aunt was not the same as a mother.

One by one the fishing vessels were coming through the Veere Gap, looming larger by the minute, and sea gulls flew around them, white and circling. The chugging of the engines carrried clearly.

Machiel set his cap on the back of his head. It still didn't fit and he'd have to grow into it. He made a face at a sea gull which skimmed swishing past his ear. He hitched up the belt of his blue overalls. All the boys wore overalls like that after school hours. But they didn't have caps like his; he was the only one who did.

"The *Ve 13* has reached the factory wharf already!" someone behind him yelled. Wolfert and Joris sauntered toward the quay. Tannie followed forlornly, leaving only Andries and Machiel behind.

"What about that boy we saw?" Andries asked.

"Hm," said Machiel. He was thinking of Moei Katrina and of the farm in southern Flanders where she and his mother had lived when they were girls. Now his mother was gone—drowned just like that—suddenly. Was that why Moei Katrina was so set against anything connected with the sea?

"It's just a matter of time," she had said not long ago. She was referring to the new dam which would force him to choose another trade.

"He's stuck-up. You can see that right off!" Andries said with emphasis.

"Oh, well . . ." Machiel said absently. He felt you must never say exactly what you thought. The grownups never did. At most, when someone tried to put them on the spot about their opinions they would say, "Well, what do you expect me to say?" or "Well, sure," which might mean anything at all.

But it certainly seemed true that the new boy had something to do with the dam. Without thinking, Machiel repeated the familiar phrase of the last few years: "It won't come to that!" He did not know himself just what he meant by it.

"Oh, come on!" Andries disagreed indignantly. "Didn't you see the way he looked?"

"Well, yes," Machiel replied. He half wanted to go on thinking about who the boy could be, but then he didn't really, because he had heard enough talk about the dam for now. He wanted to concentrate on the ships sailing in.

And suddenly Andries stood right up on the wall. "It's the *Ve 20*!" he exclaimed. "Come on! Let's go down to the wharf!"

Machiel was furious with himself. For the second time he had been caught napping. First his younger brother Sjakie had spotted the ships, and now Andries had seen Machiel's father's.

"Well, that does it," he muttered. He jumped down off the wall and with Andries behind him ran along the gravel path by the hotel. Off to the right he could hear engines chugging, chains rattling and men's voices calling to each other. Sea gulls screamed angrily, searching for scraps. The country silence was shattered, and in high spirits the boys swung along toward the ships which now approached the wharf.

The *Ve 20* sailed in majestically, her freshly painted green and black boards gleaming in the sun. Machiel's father and his older brother Dingenis stood on deck. Aft, the hands were busy with their swabs. Machiel waited with his head cocked on one side, watching skeptically to see how Dingenis would land the ship. He was so absorbed by this that he started when someone called out right next to him, "Hi, Machiel!"

He looked up right into his father's dark eyes. "Hi," he answered, slightly embarrassed, pulling at his cap and trying to decide whether or not to tell his father about the strange boy. No—not now, he decided. He vaulted eagerly on board and looked around.

Dingenis threw the hawsers around the bollards and skillfully made fast, but his father was not watching. His eyes were on Machiel. Every afternoon the boy stood on the wharf at the very same spot, waiting for his return. Skipper Cevaal thought of Dingenis, who was already a member of the crew. He was steady, level-headed and determined, easy to understand. And Sjakie? Skipper Cevaal suddenly laughed as he thought of the roguish face and inquisitive voice of his youngest son. But Machiel. It was clear the boy brooded over many things. Skipper Cevaal followed him with his eyes. Machiel was already scooping the shrimp shells and the undersized fish from the deck with a big shovel. The carts which stood on their great wheels along the quay would bring these to the factory to be ground into fish meal. Machiel set his shovel aside for a moment to peel a shrimp, and then looked up, right into the face of his father, who pretended he hadn't been standing there watching. Skipper Cevaal yawned loudly, took off his cap, resettled it on his head, and said: "School's out early, isn't it?"

"Tomorrow our fall vacation starts, that's why." Actually, school wasn't out half early enough as far as Machiel was concerned. But then, he thought, what good would it be for school to be out earlier if he couldn't go along on his father's ship anyway? There weren't many fishermen's sons in school, and he didn't even have a real friend. Well, he thought, he did have his Uncle Meindert's son Andries, but who else was there? Joris, with his lazy face? Or that stupid Wolfert?

The teacher thought Machiel should go to Junior High next year. "You can do it," he had said more than once. And Moei Katrina wanted him to go too. She just couldn't think of a fancier place than Junior High.

Machiel tilted his nose scornfully. "I'll never go," he determined, half aloud.

"Did you say something?" Gilles, his father's mate, asked behind him.

"Nothing," Machiel answered.

Suppose he still had a mother, he thought. Would she have talked about going to Junior High all the time, like Moei Katrina? Or would she have said mysteriously, "It's just a matter of time," like Moei Katrina? What had she really meant by that? Until he had had enough of the sea and chose another trade? But she ought to know better than that. As long as he could remember he had been going on board the ship to help. What else could he possibly want to be but a fisherman? One of his greatest disappointments right now was that he was hardly ever allowed on board at night. Well, only during vacation . . .

What did his father really think of it all, he wondered. And of the dam? He wished his mother was still alive. He remembered her even though he had been very young when the flood came. His mother would surely have talked to him a little more than his father did. And his father was always away.

The boat rocked unexpectedly. Skipper Cevaal interrupted

Machiel's thoughts: "Once you're on board you'll be able to take care of the carrying for me, won't you?" Then he walked away, a basket between his big hands. Later, Machiel thought, he would have his own ship. And Sjakie could come with him. And Dingenis could keep sailing with Father. Later . . . one more year before he would go out with the ships.

Machiel turned around and looked up from the water's edge at the peaked red roofs of the houses. All the guidebooks said Veere was one of the prettiest small towns in the country. Many strangers came, especially in the summer, to see how beautiful it was. Sometimes painters would sit along the quay, and among the painters and writers there were some who had never left again but had bought houses and settled there.

The tourists always wanted to go sailing, but his father didn't care for that. "No strangers on my boat," he said flatly. He didn't like talking, and the tourists talked all the time.

Skipper Cevaal stood in the fish auction hall, but he heard little of the bawling shouts all around him, or of the sharp commands of the foreman beneath the clock. Funny, he thought, how it could suddenly strike you that your children were becoming grown-up. As a fisherman you didn't have much time for them. You left each night, and when you got home, sometimes as late as six the next evening, people often came over, or things had to be taken care of before you left again at two in the morning. And recently there had been all those meetings . . .

He finished his business quickly, then turned back toward the quay. Between the curtains of nets he saw the dark figure of Machiel spreading the nets out on the deck to look for holes. Just look at that frown between his eyes! What could the boy be thinking about? He was alone so often. No mother, and

Moei Katrina wasn't getting any younger. Skipper Cevaal sighed, and then he coughed discreetly to warn Machiel of his approach. The quay was quieter now; the deck hands sat chatting a few boats farther on. Machiel's father grasped a spool of thread, just to have something in his hands.

"Your last year of school, isn't it?"

Machiel looked up. "Yes."

"Do you still want to go to fishing school in September?"

Machiel put his net down uneasily. Was his father going to start in too? "Why do you ask?"

"Well, the teacher said recently that your report cards . . . and now the dam . . ." Skipper Cevaal looked sidelong at his son, and Machiel caught his glance. He sighed with relief; his father's eyes were twinkling with fun, and all at once a warm intimacy sprang up between them.

"Tell me, Father. Maybe the dam won't go through after all. Uncle Meindert says that if they put a sluice gate in . . ."

But Machiel's father never minced words. "No, son," he said firmly. "They won't."

"Then we *will* have to leave Veere," Machiel moaned.

"If we have to, we will. We'll simply sail from Colijnsplaat."

"A plan like that won't come off so easily!" Machiel did not notice himself that he was using his uncle's words. Skipper Cevaal just smiled, very calmly.

"There is no other way. These are things in life people simply have to accept."

How firm and quiet Father is, Machiel thought. And suddenly he felt strongly how much he loved his father. After all, Machiel thought to himself, talking isn't everything.

"A strange boy from the Waterworks Authority was on the pier today," he said carelessly.

"Yes, more and more new people are coming in and bringing their families." Skipper Cevaal paused, then said, "Tell me, Machiel . . . How old were you when you came along for the first time, that night?"

"Five!" Machiel answered promptly. Would he ever forget the night when he had crept secretly on board? How frightened he had been the next day when they approached Veere! From the distance he had glimpsed his mother's white cap and her wide, black skirt. "Was there ever anyone just like you!" she had scolded in her Flanders accent, so different from the local speech. His father had just stood by, his great hands hanging almost to his knees.

"Even when you were only four you were already fooling around on the ship. You sorted out all the crayfish and starfish from among the shrimp." Machiel heard his father laughing softly. "I think you'll have to come along with me again sometimes, with Andries. It won't be long before . . ."

Suddenly Sjakie's shrill voice was heard shouting: "Machiel! Machieeeeel! Moei Katrina says if you don't come right now you won't get anything to eat!" Panting furiously, the little boy came dashing up, his father's enormous cap engulfing his head. He rushed full tilt into Skipper Cevaal, who caught his youngest son in his stride and swung him high above his head until the child crowed with delight. Together the three strode on to the house on the Market Square.

2
A NIGHT AT SEA

"Tonight, Father?" Machiel waited for his father's answer, and glanced at his friend Andries.

Skipper Cevaal looked up from his newspaper at his excited son. "Tonight what?" he asked innocently.

Machiel looked imploringly at the heavens, shrugged his shoulders, and sighed. Really, adults were impossible when they made fun of you, he thought. But his father just kept reading, and Machiel and Andries waited.

"Oh, *you* know!" Machiel finally exploded impatiently.

"Doesn't vacation begin tomorrow?" Skipper Cevaal asked slowly. He looked at the boys over the rim of his coffee cup. He wrinkled his forehead and appeared to be thinking deeply. "Oh, yes, I remember now. You have nothing to do—you'll be bored. Hm, let's see . . ." Silence. Andries coughed discreetly; Machiel shuffled his feet in his impatience. Suddenly, just as the tension was getting to be more than the boys could stand, Dingenis's deep laughter sounded behind Machiel, and even Moei Katrina could not suppress a snicker.

"Of course, if *I* had anything to do with it . . ." she began, but Skipper Cevaal was carefully scratching his head, as if he'd forgotten something.

"Oh, yes! Didn't you want to come along with me or something? Wasn't that it?"

"Oh, you remember! I've told you over and over!" Machiel exclaimed. "But you just sit there reading your old newspaper!"

"No kidding!" his father answered in mock astonishment. "Well, now that you mention it, Machiel, I seem to remember something about it after all . . ."

"Got you again, Machiel!" Dingenis suddenly laughed in delight, and as though a starting gun had been fired, Machiel and Andries fell on Skipper Cevaal, their fists pounding his broad back; Andries even managed to get him to start wrestling with them. There was such a racket in the room that the walls shook.

"Hey! Watch out!" Moei Katrina yelled over the tumult, and Skipper Cevaal dropped back into his chair, puffing and snorting.

"Well, Dingenis, what do you think?" he asked. "Do we have enough work for four people tonight?"

"Five," Dingenis said, correcting him. "There's you and me and Gilles and . . ."

"Five," Skipper Cevaal repeated, with a wink at Andries, who broke into a rare, broad grin.

"What time are we leaving?" Machiel asked.

"Oh, we've got time," his father said, calmly putting his feet up on a stool and opening his paper again. But Moei Katrina was just coming into the room, and instead of the usual two sandwiches, she had four in her hands.

"Here, I've made two more," she said grudgingly. "Not that I approve of children going to sea so young. But nobody ever asks me anything!"

The boys were so delighted that they just let her "children" pass, but Skipper Cevaal said slyly: "You come along too, Katrina." Andries practically choked on his coffee, and Machiel grabbed the paper from his father's hand, folded it, and put it on Moei Katrina's head.

"Oh, go on! You're crazy!" the old lady grumbled. Her wrinkled face beneath the paper hat looked so funny that even Skipper Cevaal and Dingenis had to laugh. Machiel looked at Andries. He knew very well why Andries had told him that he would like to come along on the *Ve 20* the first night of the vacation.

"Of course, I can always go with my own father," he had said, trying to appear as if he didn't care one way or another. "But it's more fun to be on a ship together, isn't it?"

He had not mentioned how hard it was to talk to his own father, but Machiel understood. Skipper Domisse was probably the same on board ship as he was at home with Andries and his older brother Jacob. And on a ship it was impossible to stay out of one another's way.

"We've got two hands, anyway, besides Jacob," Andries had added, anxious not to let Machiel think Skipper Cevaal's ship was better than the *Ve 13*.

"Of course," Machiel had replied. It couldn't be much fun to have your father always angry, always grumbling about the dam. Surely there must be other things in the world to talk about.

Moei Katrina looked at Machiel, and she gripped his shoulders with her thin hands as she inspected him from head to toe.

"If you're going with your father, you're going to put on your heavy socks. And your long underwear. And your boots, hear?"

His face red, Machiel shook himself free, knowing that

Andries was grinning broadly behind him. What must he be thinking! As if Machiel were five years old!

"What time are we leaving then?" Machiel asked again. "Because Andries has to get ready . . ."

"Let's see what the tide is going to be like." Skipper Cevaal went off to find out, but Dingenis said, "Go ahead, Andries. You can still catch a snooze. We'll call you." Andries took off noisily, and Moei Katrina began rattling bottles of milk through the hall.

For Father, Machiel thought. For *us,* he corrected himself. He looked curiously at his aunt's wide Cadzand skirt, so different from those of Veere or Tholen, and at the square cap which fitted snugly about her face in white pleats. He looked at her wrinkled hands. If she hadn't come along after the great flood . . . had that really been seven years ago?

Drowned in the flood. Why, Machiel wondered, did his mother just happen to be visiting his Aunt Sanne in North Beveland then? Here in Veere no one had drowned. He shivered suddenly, and his teeth began to chatter.

"You'd better get off to bed," Moei Katrina said.

"I'm going," Machiel answered loudly.

"Sleep tight," Dingenis called.

Machiel waved at Moei Katrina as he passed and clattered up the stairs. He stamped his feet like a man's in the hallway. Then he came back quickly to stick his head through the door again. "You'll call, won't you, Father?"

"Yes, son. Rest easy," his father said quietly. His brown eyes met his son's blue-gray ones for a moment and held them. On the stairs, Machiel loudly whistled a single note of pure delight.

Father read an awful lot of newspapers these days, Machiel thought. So did Dingenis. Were they all full of news about the dam, he wondered. If you wanted to build a dam right across a current, would you have to draw a diagram first? Would the wind be strong tonight? Would Andries . . .

At two o'clock Machiel was so fast asleep his father could hardly wake him. "Andries is downstairs already. But if you'd rather . . ."

Machiel was on his feet. "My cap," he mumbled sleepily. He found it in the darkness, put it firmly on his head, drew his boots on and stumbled down the stairs.

They all walked together down the dark, deserted streets, and new figures emerged from side streets to join them. Except for the muted talk of the fishermen and the noise of the sea, Veere slept and was silent.

"Great, isn't it?" Andries whispered. Ahead of them the harbor lights twinkled; here and there an engine started up. Another one. Another. By the time they reached the quay there were at least twenty or thirty engines going. One by one the black cutters pushed off from the wall and put out to sea.

The powerful searchlights of the *Ve 20* bored through the pitch darkness above the water. Now and then the light picked up two or three ships ahead of them. A snow flurry whirled across the sea, and Andries hunched himself securely into the heavy windbreaker his mother had handed him at the last minute.

The ships always vied with each other to get to the fishing grounds first. Machiel turned around and observed, "Four ahead of us!"

Andries nodded, remembered that in the darkness Machiel could not see him, and said: "Just wait!"

"We've reached the Vrouwen polder already!" Andries cried as the light gleamed again. "Hey! Did you see the dike? Didn't know we'd come this far!"

"What?" Machiel called back. Andries growled out something unintelligible, and the black night covered everything like a blanket again. The water smashed against the ship with thundering force. With each new wave the wood creaked all over the ship. The boys had to hold on tight not to be washed overboard.

"Do you remember that crazy tourist kid who wouldn't believe that water could destroy houses and break dikes?" Andries yelled above the wind. "She said, 'Water is so thin!'" He snapped his fingers scornfully.

"She ought to be here tonight!" Machiel shouted back. "She'd have to eat her words. Remember she asked us if the ships had names?"

Andries stuck up his nose. Of course the ships had names, like the *Stella Maris,* or the *Saint Joan.* But nobody ever used them. *Ve 20* or *Arn 16* was quite enough to identify any ship.

"We're out of the harbor," said Andries. Contentedly they hung on the railing, swaying with the ship's motion. Inside, voices crackled over the radio on a special fisherman's frequency. The lighthouses flung their distant lights in huge arcs across the sky and the dark water.

"How many ahead of us now?" Machiel asked.

"Four. But they left before us. We're ahead. We'll be at the fishing grounds in half an hour."

We, thought Machiel warmly. Tonight Andries regarded the *Ve 20* as his own ship.

"The sea's pretty wild!" boomed a voice right at their ears.

Machiel started, but then he laughed above the roar of the wind and waves. Imagine Gilles, Father's old hand, calling this wild! Of course he was only doing it to give them the feeling they were weathering a really rough sea.

"It's okay," Machiel answered jauntily. Andries even let go of the railing.

"Hold tight, Andries!" Skipper Cevaal's knife-sharp voice cut in suddenly from the cockpit. "No fooling around, understand?"

"Yes, uncle," Andries replied.

Then, before they knew it, they had reached the fishing grounds, and the boys were caught up in the activity all around.

The trawlers were thrown overboard. Half an hour later the signal was given for the first haul. Andries looked at the spot where his friend had stood just a moment before, and grinned. How did Machiel manage to be so slow moving at school and so lightning fast on board! Machiel bounded about, helped ready the strainer which separated the fish by size and brought the furnace up to the proper temperature.

"Everything all right?" Skipper Cevaal shouted against the wind.

"Yes, uncle," Andries yelled back, working industriously. He felt he had been let off lightly by Skipper Cevaal, who could be stern, but never nasty like his own father. And he *had* been silly, Andries realized. More than one strong man had been swept overboard by the sea.

They worked silently in the midst of the thundering force of the wind and water. The sea threw dabs of thick, white foam across their hair. This was the life, Andries thought—everyone working together, each performing his own task. A faint smell of coffee seeped over the deck. The cook rattled the cups, and fragments of news items came from the cabin. The skipper was talking to another skipper far away:

". . . didn't catch anything . . . try again now . . . not much yet . . . did you say seasick?"

"Did you catch that? Some of the others don't want to go on," Machiel said.

"Who doesn't?" Andries's voice was suddenly thin.

"The fishermen. They want to go back in for a while. Time is dragging for them, and they're getting seasick."

"Hm," Andries grunted, not working quite so hard any more.

"Their delicate little hands are too soft to pull in the trawlers," Machiel shouted sarcastically.

"The . . . the . . . s-s-s-sea isn't getting any calmer." Andries's face turned green under the lantern light, and suddenly he lunged for the railing. Was he really going to . . . ? Quickly Machiel looked away. He didn't enjoy having people watch him at such a time, and even if you were raised on the sea you could get sick sometimes. Andries was coming back, looking embarrassed.

No one saw, Machiel wanted to tell him, but just then a powerful voice shouted, "Haul away!"

There was a flurry and bustle as winches pulled the nets on board. Suddenly everything came to life, and Machiel just barely had time to glance at Andries. His face had cleared, and when the trawlers were emptied on the deck his seasickness had been forgotten.

Quick as lightning the hands secured the nets and threw them overboard again. Crabs scuttled all over the deck, and an eel slithered between Machiel's feet.

"Full steam ahead!" came the command, and they started

back to the spot where they had made their first cast. Skipper Cevaal was at the tiller, Machiel whistled off key, and Andries took off midships where Gilles sat among the catch. The old man picked up an enormous lobster and put it aside. "Could have been better," he said disappointedly. "You have to coax a ship along as if she were your girl friend."

Machiel roared with laughter, but Andries tried to console Gilles: "It must be the storm."

"Storm? What storm?" The old seaman looked up, and his eyes blinked slowly in time with the motion of the ship. "I've seen much worse." His words were nearly lost in the howling wind.

And that's the man who just got through telling us the sea's pretty wild! Machiel recalled and chuckled to himself.

"Tell us about a real storm," Andries begged.

"Well now, if I were to tell you all about it . . ."

The boys were silent. They had long ago learned that if Gilles had a story to tell he couldn't be rushed. Andries coughed impatiently, but Machiel set to work deftly cleaning the shrimp.

"Tell us about the English ship again."

"Oh, yes," said Gilles. Carefully he plucked a couple of shrimp from the heap. A crab sidled quickly away, and Gilles watched it for a moment. His fingers were still in the net, and Machiel poked Andries to keep him quiet, for if anyone spoke it would break Gilles's train of thought.

"When I was twelve . . ." The boys heard nothing but the voice of the old fisherman; they no longer even saw the shrimp, slipping through their fingers.

"Twelve . . ." the old man repeated heavily. ". . . that was long ago. There was a storm in the Veere Gap. A spring tide and nor'westerly. An English ship was in trouble, a beautiful four-master, the kind you don't see any more in these days. The men had all been taken off—most of them anyway. No one could get anywhere near the ship any more."

"Were you there, Gilles?" Andries asked excitedly.

"No, we watched from a distance." The old voice sounded regretful. "Then old Arjaan's uncle, who wasn't old himself then, took his rowboat—yes, mind you—his rowboat—out into the ferocious waves. Those waves were high as houses! Well, he was always a bit . . . what shall I say . . . a bit peculiar. Lived all alone by the dike. He just took right off for the ship. Did he expect to be able to rescue someone, or was he just curious? No one will ever know. He was never seen again."

Andries had stopped working and was staring into the distance as if he could see the stricken ship. Machiel waited quietly for the end of the story. Then Andries turned and asked, "But the ship? The English merchantman? Was she saved?"

"Are you kidding?" Gilles asked. "In a storm like that? True, six sailors were rescued by our ships. England even awarded us a medal. But . . ."

"What about Arjaan's uncle?"

"Never saw him or his rowboat again!" Gilles stood up, abruptly ending the conversation, but Machiel couldn't get his mind off it. Just think of all the secrets lying beneath the hull of their ship. If you could see deep down into the water . . . treasures . . . drowned sailors . . .

As though Andries read his thoughts he broke in: "Maybe they'll find him now when the Veere Gap is closed."

Machiel could have strangled his friend. Why couldn't he keep his mouth shut? You simply didn't talk about the dam here on board his father's ship. Neither Skipper Cevaal nor the hands ever did. "There's been quite enough talk about the dam," was all his father would say.

But Gilles nodded. "Could be you're right," he said slowly.

To change the subject, Machiel asked, "How old were you when you first went to sea, Gilles?"

"Eleven," he said.

"Just about my age."

"Yes, just about your age. But you've had a soft and sheltered life compared to all we had to go through. Was it cold sometimes! Not everything was better in those days . . ." his voice trailed off.

"Go on," Machiel said urgently.

"I started out on my father's sailing vessel. That's rather different from your smelly little motorboats here . . ."

"Oh, come on—little motorboats!" Andries protested. "Hey!" he cried as a huge wave slapped the ship and the boys grabbed at Gilles's leg for support.

The old man grinned. "Sailing isn't a bit like just turning a couple of knobs and pulling a couple of handles. You manned the ropes all night and at the same time you had to be sure the winches would hold the nets. You couldn't just sit around wasting time like we're doing now."

Machiel was aware, though, that the old man worked steadily cleaning shrimp as he spoke, never missing a single bit of shell.

"Now we'll rinse them. You want to know if I was a regular crew member in those days? Sure. I was the cook." The boys nodded. Most youngsters started out that way. "One thing follows another, and suddenly you're a fisherman."

Some of the shrimp were already cooking in the pot, and there was more light now, too. The wind brought the sound of their names being called from the forecastle, and soon they were chewing pieces of bread and drinking coffee inside with the others. Coffee never tastes or smells as good as it does at sea on a cold, windy night, Machiel thought. Dingenis rolled a cigarette between his fingers, and Gilles ate a plum. It was as comfortable and cozy as any home—in fact, it *was* a home, a little house on the sea. Machiel sighed contentedly.

"Here, take a pot of coffee up to the skipper," Dingenis ordered. Proudly the boy carried the steaming kettle to his father, who was standing at the helm. Gilles and Andries came with him.

"Take over," Skipper Cevaal said carelessly to Machiel. He gasped, and almost reverently he took the wheel. He planted himself in his father's footsteps and stared ahead intently.

"Better than school, isn't it, son?"

"I'll say!"

Machiel heard his father laughing softly. "Well it won't be long before you're a crew member for good. Now get Andries to help you throw out the bobber."

The bobber was a sort of testing net which would tell how many shrimp you could expect to catch in the next cast. Andries threw it overboard, they waited five minutes, then Machiel hauled it in. They had been through the ritual so many times they could do it all without saying a word to each other.

"Exactly sixty," Machiel said, bracing himself against the side of the dancing ship. "Not bad, huh, Gilles?"

"We'll see. Try it again." Now Andries counted, and this time there were sixty-seven shrimp in the net.

"Last cast!" came the order from the rear of the ship.

Now, as though he had never been interrupted, Gilles took up the thread of his story: "And when my father died, I became the skipper of my mother's ship. That was in the thirties. Now I'm your father's second mate, I sold my ship."

"Why?" Andries asked. Machiel had never quite dared ask the question point blank, but he couldn't understand any better than Andries why anyone would want to sell a ship. Most people were so proud to be able to own one.

"Why? Because I didn't trust her any more." Gilles spat a jet of tobacco juice into the water.

"Haul the nets!" came the command, and Gilles was gone. For hours the boys sorted and sieved, examined the fish, cleaned, cooked and chilled them. Suddenly Andries wondered aloud: "What did Gilles mean, why did he sell his ship?"

Gilles overheard him, wiped his hand over his sweaty face and said: "You don't get anything for nothing. A lot of work goes into producing a hundred pound basket of shrimp. Why did I sell my ship?" He glowered at the boys. "Well, I've told you already. Because of the Delta Plan. It's going to mean an awful lot of trouble for us fishermen."

Just then Machiel's father walked past. He must have caught Gilles's last words, for he looked sharply at the man, but all he said was: "There's coffee below."

Gilles still stood staring in the direction of the Vrouwen polder. "Won't be long now. Even before you ever get on board it'll be shut tight. And Veere will be imprisoned behind the caissons."

"*I'll* tell you something! They say . . ." Andries began shrilly. Machiel looked at Gilles's gray head tilted curiously toward Andries. The boy was busily pulling something out of his jacket. "They say a movie maker is coming to town. Here, I've got . . ." Nervously he pulled a scrap of newspaper out of his pocket and unfolded it.

"What's that? Give it to me," Gilles demanded.

But Andries was already reading: "The Government has awarded Bert Haanstra a contract to make a color film of the closing this spring of the Veere Gap. Mr. Haanstra and his co-workers are to begin filming in February."

Triumphantly, Andries looked at Machiel, then hid the paper again carefully. He probably intends to make a fuss with it at school, Machiel thought. He was uneasy—Gilles looked so annoyed, his father so threatening and now Andries frightened him with his intensity.

"This fellow will be coming here to film something which can never be filmed again!" Andries exclaimed. "He'll be here in February. You can still get through there all right now, but . . ." he nodded wordlessly port side, in the direction of Kamperland on North Beveland. Machiel did not like to look at Kamperland—what was the point of thinking of floods again? He deliberately looked to starboard, but there, just as at Kamperland, lay the broad, bent pieces of dike. Machiel was fascinated. By daylight everything looked awfully close. Little crooked green houses were strewn helter-skelter on the distant beach. People from the Waterworks Authority lived in them, Dingenis had told him—probably the new boy too. How did they build dikes, anyway? What exactly did they have to do?

The ships were turning in to the Veere Gap. Gilles spat the pit of his plum into the water and sighed heavily. "Madness. Sheer madness."

"Don't be such a bore about it, Gilles. Time enough when it's done and finished," Skipper Cevaal said coldly. His tone allowed no further argument, and Dingenis turned to look at the boys with a threat in his eyes.

"Don't you ever again . . ." he warned Andries as the skipper's voice broke in short and sharp: "Take over, Dingenis, and set the course for Veere."

The dam was not mentioned again, though Andries did

manage to mutter, "Huh," and then follow it softly with ". . . and I tell you those people are coming . . ." Machiel gave him a warning shove.

Veere lay before them like the illustration in their textbooks, the huge church looming behind the delicate Town Hall Tower. Tall houses lined the quay; the Campveerse Tower stood off to the left, thick and massive. It was high tide. Usually they would be sitting along the quay waiting for this moment. Would the others be there?

"Pssst!" Andries hissed, quite forgetting his scolding. "There's Wolfert and the rest of them!" Both boys stood even straighter, and Andries took his hand off the railing. The ships entered the harbor.

3
THE MOVIE

"I say it's a shame and it's got to be stopped!"

Andries's voice filled the classroom, and all heads turned toward him curiously. It was the Monday after the fall vacation, and Mr. Risseeuw, the teacher, had just left the room. Wolfert knew why. "A stranger has just come in," he said, "but I couldn't see who it was." He didn't mention that the teacher had chased him back into the classroom when he stuck his head out to see what was going on.

"Like an old biddy," Machiel grumbled to himself.

"Hey, Andries!" Wolfert yelled. But Andries wasn't listening at all. He had just told the news about the movie maker and was busy getting all the comments. Some found the whole idea a welcome change; others were just indifferent. There were always tourists with tripods and cameras around, and there probably always would be. Andries thought smugly, only Machiel and I—yes, and Tannie—actually understand exactly what it all means.

"Well, that's all we need," Tannie groaned.

"In the first place I don't know what you're getting all upset about," her brother Wolfert said, "and in the second place I don't know what's so special about a movie."

Tannie didn't even give him a chance to finish. "As if we haven't got enough problems, they're going to make a production out of us!"

Five or six pupils started clamoring about productions and performances and all the pros and cons of filming in Veere.

"Are you going to let me talk or not?" Andries demanded indignantly over the hubbub.

"*You* say something, Machiel," Tannie begged.

"It's just a movie!" Machiel said mildly. But now Tannie and Andries joined against him. Andries climbed right up on the bench in his excitement, and Tannie bounced up and down, punctuating each threatening sentence.

The boy shook his finger angrily in Machiel's face. "You know as well as I do it's not the same as the Americans or the Germans making a silly travelog. This is going to be a *real* film. This one is going to be made here because pretty soon they won't be *able* to make it here. Like a peepshow! They'll show our fathers sailing out of the harbor for the very last time. Going off to Colijn!"

"Well, Colijn's good farm country," Wolfert interrupted. "My father says . . ."

"You leave your father out of this!" Andries screamed, and Tannie nodded in agreement. Machiel burst out laughing. What a funny girl! She sometimes seemed to forget that Wolfert's father was her father too! But Andries thought Machiel was laughing at him and got furious.

"Don't stand there laughing like an idiot! You . . . oh, well . . ." he trailed off, cooling down.

"You're right," Machiel said quietly.

Andries went on: "The film is going to be shown in movie houses all over the country." He looked around proudly. He was having a field day, making a full-scale speech, everyone listening eagerly to him.

"You mean," Joris said in his slow way, "that it will all be shown in the movie? I mean of course it'll show Veere and all that . . . but all the people too? And the boats . . . and . . . all of us . . . and all the rest of it?"

"Yes!" Andries barked. "What did you expect?"

"Then maybe a movie isn't such a bad idea," Joris remarked, nodding his head a couple of times. Tannie immediately flew at him in a fury, hammering his back with her fists. Bewildered, Joris could only protest: "Hey! Can't I even say what I think?"

"Leave him alone," Andries ordered. But Tannie wouldn't stop.

"Doesn't anyone here care that they're going to make fools of all the fishermen?"

"Make fools of them?" Joris asked.

"Absolute fools," Andries agreed. "They want to film the fishing fleet going out for the last time. All the ships will be there. And all the fishermen. And their families. And everyone will get a chance to stand and gape at them." He was getting all wound up again.

"Yes. Do you really think it's going to be a holiday for those poor people?" Tannie demanded.

"Oh, come on! You'd think you owned a shrimp boat yourself," her brother teased.

"Oh, shut your mouth!" Machiel interrupted. Andries turned around, surprised and grateful for this assistance. "If they see your ugly mug on the film they'll scrap the whole thing anyway," Machiel added, drawing a laugh from the class. Wolfert, however, turned beet-red, and a real fight was not far off.

"It's always the dam that causes trouble around here," Adriana Dingemanse said from her corner near the window. She was a rather shy girl and everyone looked surprised when she spoke. Silence was restored.

"She's right," Machiel agreed. "If it wasn't for the dam . . ."

"Well, what do you want?" Wolfert yelled. "The dam is there—or at least it's going to be. They're just going to go right through with their plans, and there isn't a thing we can do about it."

"Who are you talking about?" Machiel demanded coldly.

"The Waterworks people, of course."

"They've got nothing to do with the movie, you idiot!"

The shouting started up again, and Tannie wailed above the din: "Why doesn't anyone ever *do* anything!"

"What do *you* care! *You* don't have to move to Colijn!" Wolfert screamed.

"What do you want to do? About what?" Machiel asked Tannie.

"Well, everything. The dam . . . and . . . the movie . . ." But suddenly Tannie slumped back into her seat. "Of course that's impossible," she said softly.

"I . . . I . . ." Tannie began again. "I *don't* have anything to do with it, of course. But if they . . . if people . . . I know the fishermen's wives will be crying," she finished. She looked up shyly, but the boys were nodding in agreement.

"And all that will be caught on film. Every stranger will see it."

Her helpless words had achieved what all Andries's shouting

never could. Clumsily Machiel said: "Don't say that—I mean— that nothing is going to be done. My father says there's a committee . . ."

Tannie sniffled into her handkerchief. "That's grownups again; children don't even count. And what can you expect of grownups?"

They thought it over silently, and Joris agreed: "She's right, you know. Have you ever heard grownups discussing a plan?"

"Only the Delta Plan," Tannie moaned.

"Oh, come off it! It's going to be great fun," Wolfert still maintained stoutly. "I'm going to make sure I'm in it. On television . . ." No one even listened. Furiously he screamed, "All *right!* Then *you* tell me how you're going to stop it!"

"Want to bet I can?" Andries's brown eyes sparkled, and his voice was so mysterious that everyone looked at him curiously. Quickly, they formed a circle around him and Machiel. Andries looked about cautiously, dropped his voice to a whisper, and put his finger on his lips. "When the man comes to Veere, of course he'll go . . ."

Suddenly, Wolfert cried, "Pssst! Teacher!" Andries almost attacked him, sure that he was teasing, but Wolfert insisted, "It *is* the teacher! He's coming down the hall! He's got the new boy with him."

Silently they turned their faces toward the glass pane in the classroom door.

Andries barely had time to hiss, "This afternoon! The Campveerse Tower!"

The door opened slowly.

4
THE DELTA PROJECT

THE first thing the new boy saw was the heads bent toward one another hiding a secret from him. He would remember that picture for a long time.

Unconsciously, he stuck his chin out and regarded the group just as coldly as he could. He knew it was going to be the same thing all over again: kids always looked at him as though he were an Eskimo or something. There was the one he'd noticed at the Tower wearing the funny cap. Nothing unusual about him now, without the cap. Indifferently, the boy looked away and waited for the teacher to assign him to a seat.

The class stared, a bit startled by the sudden appearance of the teacher and the strange boy, a bit guilty, too, at the way they were standing like conspirators around Andries's desk, and perhaps a bit hostile, waiting as they always did with a stranger to see what he would turn out to be like. They certainly wouldn't forget that this boy was a "Waterworks Authority brat."

The teacher did not need to say a word; one by one the children returned to their desks.

Machiel saw the fleeting look the stranger gave him and knew that he had been recognized. He felt himself turning red. Andries was right, he told himself—the boy did look stuck-up. No—arrogant—that was the word. Still . . . Suddenly Machiel thought of Colijn, and for the first time the name had real meaning for him. Colijn meant a strange harbor for his father, but for him and for Andries, it meant a new school. He'd find himself in the same fix as this boy, being led by a new teacher into a classroom full of strangers. At that moment, Machiel made up his mind to get along with the new boy, Waterworks Authority or no.

Mr. Risseeuw felt the hostility in the classroom, caught the children's sidelong glances, and knew they wouldn't be looking at an ordinary stranger quite like that. But he merely said, "Wolfert, will you move to the rear desk for a while, please? It's quieter there. Then Allard van Beusekom can get used to *my* face before he starts on yours!" He grinned broadly, and Machiel was amused. What a sly fox this teacher was! Machiel almost laughed out loud when he caught sight of Wolfert's angry expression as he packed up his things to move.

"Allard, yet," Andries muttered. "And Van Beusekom. Far cry from decent fishermen's names like Joris and Jacob and Machieltje. But of course we have to realize their lordships have come to dispossess the fishermen."

Turning to answer, Machiel caught Tannie's look. She was staring so hard at the new boy's face that Machiel could hardly suppress a grin.

"You think it's a laughing matter?" Andries hissed furiously. "Just you wait. I'll . . ."

"All done?" the teacher cut in. "You'll have a chance to gape at the new boy later. Isn't that the way it always is? I remember my own schooldays."

Judging from Mr. Risseeuw's joking tone, the matter didn't really seem very serious, but some resentment lingered in the classroom. What business did this stranger have coming here, with his indifferent manner and his hair all slicked down? He was tall, too. Machiel stole a glance at his own legs beneath the bench. "Good Zeeland sea legs," Moei Katrina always said of them. But they certainly weren't long. Well. Didn't he have anything better to worry about? For instance, the dam this boy's father and those other men were about to build. Andries was right, after all . . .

Machiel's thoughts were far away when Allard's name suddenly rang through the room, and he realized that the teacher had long since started the lesson.

". . . and the worst part of it is that people generally don't even know what they're angry about. Take the Delta Plan. People here just criticize it. But do you think any of them have the slightest idea what it really is? Not at all."

"Dam closed, fishermen gone," Andries muttered.

"All the little islands will be closed off with dams. And the Waterworks Authority is planning to clear the people off," Wolfert hissed.

"And they certainly don't know anything about the Three-Island Plan," the teacher continued.

"Dams are dams," Andries growled.

"Now hold your tongues, all of you!" Mr. Risseeuw suddenly ordered, so loudly that even Andries shot straight up in his seat. A warning note sounded in his voice, and the children found themselves compelled to listen.

Heads to one side, they no longer heard the November storm that raged through the trees outside. Instead they saw landscapes changing shape very slowly through the ages. Just as you don't notice changes in people you see every day, Mr.

Risseeuw was telling the class, you aren't able to see the minute alterations being made in the coast line each day. Such changes become obvious only after two or three hundreds of years. It is hard to imagine such development, but the teacher pointed to a map on the wall so that they could see clearly.

Ages ago the seas had been lower, and colder, too. Slowly the temperature rose; the ice caps retreated northward, and the melting waters raised the sea level toward the south, so that nine thousand years ago, the North Sea overflowed the entire coast of Holland.

Then, only seven thousand years ago, enormous pressure caused the water to break through the land between Dover, in England, and Calais, in France. Suddenly the North Sea was linked with the Atlantic Ocean. The roaring waters drew sand along in their wake, piling it up into protective dunes on the Dutch coast. Then, in the first century A.D. ramparts were built to defend the remaining land against the sea.

Several hundred years later the coast line of Holland was ripped off violently to form Zeeland and the South Holland islands. The Rhine and the Meuse and the Schelde flowed to the sea about where Rotterdam is today.

But, as the children all knew, sand shifts constantly with the movement of the sea. The Calais Narrows became choked up again. And the wild sea, hurling itself against the coast all the way to the delta region, destroyed the ancient dunes. The arms of the North Sea drew wider and wider till they drowned the whole southwest of Holland. That was in the twelfth century, and at times it looked as though the entire country would be totally destroyed. But men defied the sea.

"Do you hear?" the teacher said urgently. "It *can* be done! You don't always have to sit by like lazy duffers. Not even you!" This comment he directed to Wolfert, whose attention had long since wandered from the map. "We in Veere have been fighting the sea for eight hundred years, building and maintaining our dikes, slowly and steadily, persistently, carefully. The water is our most ancient enemy. But the outcome of the fight depends on the means we have to fight with. And now, man has taken up the challenge with his remarkable modern inventions. Before the year 2000 all the openings to the sea, except those of the Western Schelde and the Rotterdam Waterway, will be dammed shut. It *can* be done!"

After stopping for a moment, Mr. Risseeuw continued. "You can defend yourself against the sea piecemeal with dikes. But you can also launch an all-out attack by building these giant dams which will keep the sea from pouring all the way inland. You might remember that," he said, fixing their eyes with his own. "Defenses of dikes *and* an all-out attack. 'For land held is many victories won,' the saying goes, and the man who said it first, Andries Verlingh, was from Veere. They snatched the delta region from the sea. You mustn't forget that it is made up of polders, land regained from the sea. You and I are here now, but it was a terrible struggle. There have been floods that caused whole villages in North Beveland to be drowned, never to be found again. And you know as well as I do that in rough weather people in Colijn still go around inspecting the sea walls. Not surprising, when they're surrounded on all sides by water!"

From the back of the classroom came Wolfert's teasing voice: "Well, Andries and Machiel ought to be standing guard there pretty soon now!"

Mr. Risseeuw's expression did not change. "Think of Walcheren, which used to consist of seven islands. In 1300 they built a ring dike all the way around it, but there still were those terrible, deep channels through Dutch Flanders—you know, the place Machiel's aunt comes from."

Oh, now really! "Machiel's aunt!" Machiel colored and put his hands beneath his chin for support. Moei Katrina should just hear this!

"Look! Do you all see Walcheren on the map?" The teacher's voice sounded through the classroom. "Then you also see that the dikes have had to be built all the way around each island separately. Just think of all the trouble people had to go to, building and maintaining those miles of dikes! Now Allard's father has something better up his sleeve. Let's have a look."

The new boy seemed to be listening attentively, but Andries was muttering something behind his hand.

"This is the final attempt. Mine too, for that matter," Mr. Risseeuw added, grinning. "Let's go back to the Three-Island Plan to reunite the parts of the Beveland region: Walcheren and North and South Beveland. One dam that will protect all three islands is going to be built, closing the whole region off from the sea. Basically, it's the same idea as the earlier one but much easier, and it can't be improved upon. They'll build roads on these dams, and, finally, the islands will be connected. That's all I wanted to tell you today. That's it. Period."

The lecture had been quite long enough for the children, who all started clearing their throats and shuffling. But unexpectedly Andries asked: "Is all this really necessary, sir?"

Everyone was suddenly quiet. Not that one couldn't feel free to question the teacher, but this . . . Andries seemed almost surprised at his own loud voice. More quietly he continued: "My father says a harbor without ebb and flood tides is dead as a doornail."

"I see what you mean, my friend," Mr. Risseeuw answered. "But remember the dates of all the floods we've had for centuries. Learn them by heart. Think of all the things that have been destroyed by the water—men, women, children, houses, livestock . . ."

"Cars," Wolfert added.

"Cars too. And land, cities, churches and businesses. I certainly don't have to tell *you* what happened in the flood of January 1953."

No, he did not. They had been five or six years old then, but they still remembered the flood barricades in the roads. They still remembered that about a hundred and fifty breaches and holes had been knocked in the dikes of Zeeland, and that more than eight hundred people had lost their lives in the roaring waves. Thousands had had to flee their homes. They looked at Adriana Dingemanse, from the island of Schouwen. It had been worst of all there. From Adriana they looked at Machiel, who looked straight ahead. Stop staring, he thought furiously.

Mr. Risseeuw quickly continued: "That *must* not happen again. Each year the population grows, and another disaster like that would claim even more victims."

Andries wasn't about to give up yet. He looked accusingly at the new boy, and blurted out, "Yes, but . . ."

"Why are they building the dam right at Veere?" the teacher finished Andries's question. "Machiel?" The boy frowned. There it was again—he was supposed to be able to come up with an intelligent answer. Gaining time, he stammered, "Uh . . . well . . ."

"Yes, that's a very good reason," Mr. Risseeuw commented drily. Someone giggled, and Tannie coughed nervously. She couldn't stand to see Machiel embarrassed.

"For some people's safety," Machiel finally said. You couldn't go wrong with an answer like that.

"A brilliant conclusion!" The teacher's eyes glided teasingly over Machiel's face. It was impossible to put anything over on this man. Wolfert raised his hand.

Apple polisher! Machiel thought angrily.

"Because the land's getting salty." Wolfert practically fell off the bench in his eagerness.

"Great!" Andries hissed bitterly. "And the fishermen are just supposed to sit around and see what happens."

But Mr. Risseeuw merely said, "You mean as a measure against it. Whose concern is that mainly, Wolfert?"

"My father's," came the quick answer. "And—uh—the farmers'."

Someone knocked at the classroom door, and the teacher said: "Silence, all of you now. I just have to . . ."

He had no sooner disappeared down the hall than Andries turned around and shouted: "Always the farmers, isn't it?"

"You fishermen will just have to leave. And it won't be long now," Wolfert crowed triumphantly, nodding at the new boy.

"What do you mean *have* to? We'll decide for ourselves!" Andries retorted.

"Fishermen bother you?" Machiel demanded bitingly.

"Not me, but they bother my father. Little by little all his land is turning salty. It was in the *Farm News*. And just because a handful of fishermen. . . . Well, my father says so himself. You'll all just have to move, that's all there is to it." He looked at Machiel and Andries vengefully. But they weren't about to let him have the last word.

"Maybe as far as your father's concerned," Andries yelled. He would just as soon move, but that was something else again. To have to move just because Wolfert's father . . .

"In a pig's eye!" Machiel exploded.

"Then you're not really going to Colijn, Machiel?" Tannie asked hopefully.

"How would *I* know?" he answered with studied indifference. "We'll just have to wait and see." He had heard his father and his uncle say that so often that the words came to him almost automatically. "There's water in Colijn, same as here. And a school too!"

"Well, my father also says . . ." Wolfert began again.

Tannie whirled around and gave her brother a crack on the head. He reached up furiously.

"I say a farmer should mind his own business!" she cried.

"Yeah! His dungheap!" Joris drawled. Some of the children laughed, but Wolfert started on one of his real rages.

"You'll see I'm right! My father is on the Town Council and your fathers aren't. And he said . . ."

"I thought members of the Town Council weren't supposed to talk about their discussions," a voice suddenly broke in. It was the new boy who up to now had merely followed the conversation curiously and a bit mockingly. The others stared dumbfounded at this new attack on the subject.

"By thunder he's right!" Andries said loudly. "Machiel's father and mine are on the Fishermen's Council, and we never talk half as much about it."

"You keep out of this," Wolfert yelled at Allard. "Isn't it just great to have you take sides with the fishermen when we all know you people have only come to drive them out!"

"Oh, come off it! We've got other things on our minds than a handful of people around here. What nonsense," said Allard disdainfully.

"Oh, yeah? Oh, yeah?" Wolfert was out of his seat, his fists doubled in front of him, and the boys watched tensely to see what the new boy would do. Slowly Allard stood up, tall and straight. But just as Wolfert squared off, Machiel knocked his hand back with one sweep of his arm.

"Quit it!" he snapped. "He's right. It *is* nonsense!"

"Quite true," came a stern voice.

Mr. Risseeuw!

He looked sharply at the last row. "Go into the corridor and wait for me, Wolfert," he ordered.

The boy slunk off, and the teacher looked silently at Andries who sat staring down at his hands. "Those farmers never think of anything but their precious land," he mumbled, obviously embarrassed.

"And they're right, too!" Mr. Risseeuw answered sharply. "I have just one thing to say to you thoughtless chatterboxes: Wolfert can be a pain in the neck sometimes, but so can you. And he comes from a farm on which Van Borsseles have lived since 1660, and probably other farmers were there before them. Land has always been just as important as water in Walcheren, understand? They have had to fight for that land day and night, and if you had been listening before you would have known that. His father and the other farmers have just as much right to hold on to their land and defend it against the sea as you have to retain your fisheries. Whether you are fishermen or farmers or engineers, don't talk like fools. It's certainly true that the new dam will help the farmers. Not only will the land be protected from sea storms, but all the water closed in behind the dam will gradually be converted to fresh water. And the water will be like a lake, so people can swim and go sailing."

A few children snickered.

"But that's not the important thing!" Mr. Risseeuw added

quickly. "The important thing, looking at it from the farmers' point of view, is that the soil won't be endangered by salt any longer. The salty sea water will be kept out and the land will be more productive, and that helps everybody, farmers and fishermen. And now get out of here—I've had quite enough for one day!"

He stood at the door as the class scampered out. No one paid any further attention to Allard van Beusekom. Passing Wolfert sulking in the hall, Andries quickly made a face, and said, "Looks as if he'll have to be going to Colijn himself." But no one was interested in arguing any more as they thought of the teacher's set face.

"He said, 'we people of Veere,'" Tannie muttered. She was really sorry now that she had jumped on her brother like that. After all, what the teacher said was true, and not many in the class realized how proud Wolfert was of the farm and his family. Actually, she herself had never thought much about it.

"He really was mad," Joris remarked thoughtfully.

"It's all because of the fellow from the Waterworks." Andries was obstinate. "What's he doing here anyway?"

"Oh, well," Machiel said, trying to smooth things over.

Then Joris suggested, "Let's go over to the Tower and wait for the ships. And then Andries can tell us his plan for the movie people."

"Yes, let's! To the Tower!"

They ran along the quay, shrieking happily, past white painted markers and coils of rope, over the feet of a man gathering in fish, who scolded loudly after them.

"Now about those movie guys . . ." Just as Andries was about to reveal his plans for the film makers and their crew, Allard van Beusekom walked past them slowly.

"Now *there's* a picture," said Tannie under her breath. She giggled nervously, but Andries was angry at being sidetracked again.

"Well, you can say what you like," he said with a meaningful glance at Machiel, "but he's stuck-up anyway. And it's his fault and his father's that we have to put up with all this nonsense."

"Oh, stop it," Machiel pleaded. "All that fuss in class wasn't his fault. And anyway, will you go ahead and tell us your idea?"

Machiel's thoughts were in a turmoil: he was against the dam but not the new boy. His confusion made him uneasy. Tannie spoke up: "Tell us, Andries! What are you planning to do?"

5
ALLARD

The new boy, Allard van Beusekom, had started his fifth school a few hours before. Now he walked down the street alone. He felt uncomfortable and confused, and recognized a familiar inner tension. Would the other boys turn out to be nice? Would there be a couple or maybe even just one he'd be able to be friends with? "Huh!" he muttered angrily. Friend. Forget it. Even the boy he had seen by the Tower earlier, even he was one of the gang. He had just caught sight of them all running off, all looking at him with exactly the same expression in their eyes, as if to say, "What are *you* doing here?"

The teacher was all right, but what good was a friendly teacher if the boys in the class weren't going to have anything to do with you or simply stared all the time?

He had seen right away that the fat guy with the funny name had it in for him. The teacher had told him off, but that wasn't going to change Wolfert.

That's the way it always is, Allard thought despondently.

One class could look pretty much like all the others—after all, you'd expect them to stare and look you over at first—but then there would always be just one who would turn the whole bunch against you just because you were a stranger. Why had he thought things would be different in Veere from the way they had been in Hellevoetsluis or in Maastricht, or in Bruinisse or Velsen? His father had said he'd love to go back to Zeeland, and that the people were nice there. But he had clearly forgotten how it really was; he was just eager to start work on the dam.

Nice people! Sure! A bunch of ignorant farmers, and the fishermen weren't much better.

Muttering to himself, Allard reached the quay, and suddenly the glorious bright light over the sea caused him to stop. Surprised and enthralled, he gazed down the length of the quay. There was a hustle and bustle there which contrasted sharply with the quiet of the streets from which he had just come. The boy watched, fascinated. His gaze was drawn to the ships nearest him where several young men were busy stowing nets. They had taken down the pole from which the nets were hung and knelt, one on either side, a long string of huge white floats behind them like a train. They wore seaman's sweaters and berets—not caps, like that boy in his class. One had his back to Allard, his wooden shoes off. Across from him, on the other side of the pole, another man was telling a story, and everyone suddenly laughed. A few feet behind them a couple of young men lifted a basket of fish high into the air. One of them scooped something from a bucket into the pail of a boy who had just run up. Obviously one could buy fish right here at the wharf—he'd have to tell his mother about that.

Allard chuckled softly, but the man nearest him heard and

turned his head sharply. He looked narrowly at the intruder, and the other fishing boys said something rapidly under their breaths which Allard could not understand. He felt himself turning red and he angrily walked a few steps off. But then he stood his ground stubbornly: he would walk where he pleased!

Steadying himself, he put one foot on the cable which held the ship against the quay. How he'd love to be on a ship like that! The ship began to drift with the movement of the cable, and a loud voice called: "Hey! Keep off that!"

Startled, Allard jumped backward. Several people on the ship stared, grinning at him. Allard did not know who had shouted, but the boy who had bought the fish turned to look at him too.

"Hey, Waterworks!" he yelled. It was Wolfert. Now they were all looking at him, mockingly, Allard thought. Should he leave now or stay?

Wolfert bent toward the oldest of the deck hands and whispered something. The youths burst out laughing, and Allard felt himself turning red again. Brusquely, he whirled around and stamped off, past the ships, toward the fish factory. He did not realize the fishermen were laughing good-naturedly. He felt they were all against him and any stranger connected with the dam. Maybe it would have been all right on the quay if that miserable Wolfert hadn't stirred everybody up. He'd go to the jetty; at least nobody would be able to chase him off that.

Suddenly Allard heard swift steps behind him, a bucket rattled and Wolfert's familiar loud voice said, "Didn't like that, did you?"

Allard stopped dead. "Hit back," his father had told him. Well, he would . . .

"Didn't like what?" His voice was cool, as cool as his father's.

"Oh, come off it! You wanted to get on those boats."

"I don't need your old wooden tubs!" Allard snapped.

"Wooden tubs!" said Wolfert in great indignation. "That's too much! Just because you couldn't get on the ship while the hands were busy."

Pretending it was all the same to him, Allard looked right through Wolfert. What do you know! he thought—it worked. Slowly, Wolfert slunk off, his bucket banging forlornly against his fat legs. His wooden shoes clattered.

He turned around just once. "Dirty foreigner!" he shouted.

Shoulders hunched and hands in his pockets, Allard sauntered along. "Let them all go to blazes!" he muttered softly. But at the same time he wanted to belong, to be included in anything the others were planning. Would they be sitting by the Tower again?

As he walked over the cobblestones, Allard stole a glance at his shoes and trousers. He felt his sport shirt beneath his jacket. He looked pretty much like these other boys. What was it, then, that set him so clearly apart?

"It's because you don't quite belong," his mother had once told him. "And they're really a bit jealous of you. You've seen so much more than they have. You've been so many places. Villagers are like that, and I'm afraid you can't change them."

Jealous of him, Allard thought. If his parents only knew!

"Have you ever seen chickens fight a strange hen who's been put into their coop?" his father had asked. "Well, then. People are no different."

Allard had laughed a bit about the chickens, but his heart wasn't in it.

"Don't let them get you," his father had advised. "And if they make things tough for you, hit back."

Suddenly the boy turned. A thought had struck him. His teacher was okay—if a stranger openly took your side, everything would be all right. But then he wondered how his sister Celestine's first day in her fourth grade class had been. Allard walked faster; his mother would want to know all about his new school.

An orange and blue lifeboat bobbed in the little harbor near a high, narrow bridge. Left of the bridge, about fifteen minutes away, was Allard's house. It was a bit outside Veere— just like themselves, Allard thought bitterly. Far away to the right as the jetty where . . . should he go and see? He could go home. But of course his father wouldn't be there yet. He never was. But suppose he was home after all? Allard wrinkled his nose, scanning the harbor as he walked over the high bridge. People were always coming to talk to his father— contractors, managers, overseers. And they talked about the dam, about sand and cobblestones, basalt and gravel. They looked at current charts and tide tables. Ground water, ebb strength, size and slope of the dikes, sand, plumbs, stone, concrete, asphalt—Allard had heard all these words so often he could recite them in his sleep. A dike looked like a very simple thing, but even he knew that an enormous number of different calculations were necessary before building could begin. His father worked without stopping; he was always in a hurry.

Deep in his own thoughts, Allard had come to the black wooden jetty. Far to his left he could see the cranes with their crooked necks, and he knew his father was there and would stay until late tonight. Men relieved each other periodically; the work never ceased. Even at night the angular cranes swayed and dumped load after load of wet clay into the sea.

Powerful lights burned so that the work need not stop. The workmen seemed to be having a contest with the sullen sea and with the fall storms which would not wait.

Allard's thoughts went back to his class that afternoon. Those idiots. They hadn't the least idea that their own safety was at stake. His father had told him all about it before they had come to Veere, about the terrible flood seven years before. Foreigners never understand how the Dutch dared live on such a flat piece of land, below sea level in many places, on the floors of what had once been lakes and inland seas. "We Dutch are the first to be shocked when something happens," his father had said grimly. "It's a wonder no more has happened. When we build a dam to save people's skins, they get angry." He tapped his forehead significantly.

"Well, it's a pretty big thing for the fishermen, Alfred," his mother had said soothingly. Her husband looked at her face while she spoke, at the cool light reflected from the sea falling on her hair, and his expression softened.

"Oh, well," he said. Allard remembered this scene perfectly because that was what he himself always said when he knew that the other person was right. "Oh, well."

Allard realized that his father knew the fishermen would have to move, but "You have to break an egg to make an omelet," Mr. van Beusekom would always say. What could he do about it, anyway? They'd just have to fish elsewhere. The reclamation project was going like clockwork. Still . . .

Allard picked up a stick to poke at the crabs running between his feet. That boy—Machiel—he certainly didn't look like that Wolfert. He was the kind you'd want to be friends with. Even while he was thinking this, Allard knew it was impossible. Friends! he thought. Machiel would have to be

crazy. All well and good for him to come to Allard's defense
in class, but you could be sure he was sitting and plotting
with the rest of them now. Wait! he thought. He would be
able to see if he just walked down the jetty a way. He'd take
a quick look—as if he were looking at the ships and the sea.

Humming a bit off key, Allard sauntered along the jetty.
There they were. The very moment his eyes met theirs, an
unholy racket burst forth. It was directed against him, Allard
was sure. Yes, of course—there was Wolfert, swinging his
bucket of fish. He must be telling the rest of them what had
happened down by the boats. Machiel was wearing his dark
cap. Allard couldn't make out his face too well. Friends?
That would be the day! The boy didn't even care if Allard
existed! He forgot he had meant to stare at the sea, and thrust-
ing his hands in his pockets he walked off the jetty.

They *must* be laughing at me, Allard thought. What else
would they be laughing at? Besides—it was always like that.
Just once he had almost made a friend, but then they had had
to move. His father could afford to talk—he was obsessed with
his battle with the water. Allard tried to imagine his father
coming to a strange school, starting all over again for the fifth
time and being met by a bunch of grinning apes in a dump
like this. Wouldn't he just love to see that!

Allard forgot the fishing boats which had fascinated him
just a moment ago. He did not see the nets hanging on the
masts, swaying back and forth in the wind. He didn't even
hear the tune ringing out from the Town Hall bells. Disappointed and lonely, he walked home.

6
THE PLAN

ANDRIES DOMISSE's excited voice rang beneath the Camp-veerse Tower, all but drowning the shrieks of the sea gulls. He was a commanding figure, but the other children interrupted him constantly. Tannie had brought Adriana Dinge-manse, and as soon as Andries started talking about his plan, the two of them began to giggle, and that started the others off too. They were constantly interrupting Andries with a "Yes, but . . ." or "You'll never pull that off!" or "And *I* tell you . . ."

"Just don't expect us to do your dirty work!" Tannie exclaimed. They all knew Andries was great at making plans, but he was also astonishingly good at arranging the actual work so as to keep the softest jobs for himself. But Andries was quite aware they were all looking to him for guidance, so he said emphatically, "There are other ways to stop people, you know. As I started to say, the people assembled here . . ."

"Well, I wouldn't say we were assembled," Joris said carefully. "I'm just sitting here."

Quickly Machiel remarked: "Everyone sitting here is responsible for our final actions."

"That's it," Andries said. "That's the way it was in the book too."

"How did they manage to stop the dam there?" someone wanted to know.

"There wasn't any dam!"

"But you said . . ."

"I didn't say anything!" Andries yelled angrily. Several voices protested loudly, and Andries had difficulty making himself heard.

". . . all I said was they had to make a plan to blow up a bridge."

"Must have been a war story," Tannie remarked.

Andries gave her a withering look, and Tannie turned bright red. It was funny how, for all her sharp claws, Tannie could sometimes look so helpless that you just had to try and do something for her, Machiel thought. He opened his mouth to say something, but Tannie had already recovered and snapped, "Things like that don't happen in real life."

"How do you know?" Andries challenged.

"It would be too much trouble anyway," Machiel said.

"Old Arjaan himself said, 'Chuck a piece of dynamite under it.' He meant under the dam, you know." Andries's eyes were sparkling again, but then a cloud of disappointment descended. "But you've got to have a war for things like that. Then you'd find the stuff lying around everywhere, but not these days. Of course we could buy it, but . . ."

"But imagine what it would cost!" Joris interrupted.

The others simply sniffed. Only Tannie looked carefully at Joris's drawn and worried face, and suddenly she burst out:

"You all . . . you all just want to be such heroes! Dynamite yet!"

"Well, what's *your* plan?" Andries asked.

Tannie thought it over. Challenged in this way she had to be able to come up with a better suggestion.

"A . . . a telegram!"

The others stared at her puzzled.

"A telegram? To whom?"

"To the Prime Minister. Or to . . ." They were all staring at her so attentively she just had to make it good. "Well, people do that, you know. Last week I read about someone in Italy whose father gave him money for a pair of track shoes. He went and spent it all on a telegram to the President of the United States."

They were impressed and suddenly silent. Only Joris protested: "You'd be crazy to throw good money away on that." This time the others had to admit he was right. Their parents used the very same words when money was about to be spent foolishly.

"Why did the boy send the telegram?" Andries asked in his iciest tone.

"I don't know," Tannie admitted weakly. She realized they weren't going to adopt her suggestion. "It was an old newspaper . . ." Her fingers plucked nervously at her coat buttons.

"What about a letter?" Adriana piped up.

"Nobody writes letters these days," Andries said. It was true —they didn't know anyone who did.

"We could do what some people in Flanders did," Machiel said, quickly gesturing toward the sea. "They went to The Hague to ask for free ferry service over the West Schelde. My aunt told me about it herself. They had posters and demonstrated in front of the Ministry of Transportation. People do things like that, you know, when there's something they don't like going on."

He took a deep breath, cleared his throat, and pulled his cap down more firmly over his eyes. He didn't often make long speeches like that, and even Andries was surprised. But Machiel looked away as if he didn't care.

Boys always thought they knew everything, Tannie thought. Okay, she decided: no telegram, no trip to The Hague.

"So? Did they get their free ferry service?" she demanded loftily.

"Well, no . . ."

"See? I knew it!" Triumphantly, Tannie nudged Adriana. Together they looked at Machiel so coldly that he started pulling at the visor of his cap again. Girls! he thought. It would be a long time before he would stick his neck out for Tannie again.

"Think up something for yourself, then," he said angrily.

"There's Wolfert," Adriana remarked softly, hoping to change the subject, but nobody paid any attention to the boy ambling up with his pail of cod.

"What I don't understand," Joris said, "is why you're always talking about the dam. What's that got to do with the movie makers?"

The girls nodded. It was all too much for Andries.

"Oh, really! You're all so *stupid!*" he roared. It was true he'd lost his train of thought, but he didn't need someone like Joris to point it out to him.

"Oh, yeah? Then *you* explain!" Tannie cried.

"If there weren't going to be a dam, there wouldn't be any movie makers. There!" Machiel said. They quarreled about that for a while, but it was Andries who finally silenced them.

"I've got it!" he exclaimed, knocking himself on the fore-head. "The word I was looking for: Sabotage. That's what the boys in the book did."

"Has it got something to do with war again?" Tannie interrupted.

"No. Well, yes. Besides, what if it does?" Andries screamed angrily. "You're not going to sidetrack me again, do you hear?"

Tannie was so shocked she just stared at Andries, who dropped his voice to a whisper.

"To sabotage means to stop something. They couldn't blow the bridge up, they'd have been caught."

The others nodded, a bit relieved.

"But they could prevent its being used," Andries continued. "With guns!"

Joris fidgeted, and after a moment he said, "Then you might as well use dynamite."

"Come on, be reasonable. I didn't say we had to do that. All I wanted to show is that there are things that can be done. You can't unplan the Delta Plan—Tannie's right. There isn't a living soul around who could move those caissons now. And nobody's ever gotten anything done by sending telegrams. We'll find something before March thirtieth . . ."

"What's March thirtieth?" Wolfert asked.

"You ought to know by now," Machiel answered impa-tiently. "It's the day the fleet goes out for the last time." He pointed northward. "After the thirtieth not even a mouse will be able to get in or out. My father's got the date marked on a piece of paper. And that's when the movie people will shoot their film."

Wolfert put his bucket of fish down on the wall. He wished he hadn't been so stupid. "Well, if you want to do anything, you'll just have to chase those people out!" he blustered.

"Well, isn't that just what . . ."

Paying no attention to Joris's objection, Wolfert leaned all the way over the parapet and looked down into the water below. "How deep do you think the water is here?" he asked in a muffled voice.

"Oh, now look!" Tannie cried. "I won't go along with anything like that!"

"Me, either," Joris said, and Adriana murmured, "Shame on you!"

"Whisper!" Wolfert cautioned. He was delighted to have their full attention. "Who says we should take that guy and . . ." he gestured at the water. "I meant his camera, of course." His eyes glittered. He gestured again toward the water as it pounded against the wall.

Andries thought it over carefully for a minute. Then he said, "Yes, but how would you get your hands on it?"

"Impossible," Machiel said. "Those people are crazy about their cameras."

"You see? It's all so difficult."

But Andries's mind was still on the book. "I don't see why we don't . . ."

"We're a bunch of idiots!" Wolfert suddenly shouted. "We'll have to see to it there's nothing to film!"

"Whaaaat?" "But how are you going to . . ." "Ah, you're crazy!" Exclamations flew about, but they didn't faze Wolfert.

"Nothing to film," he repeated significantly.

"You mean . . ." Machiel hesitated. "There won't be any ships?"

"The ships won't sail out," Wolfert said laconically.

Andries caught his breath. "You'll have to disguise them, then," he said restraining himself. His eyes darted to the pier where dozens of masts stuck up into the sky. "How are you going to do it?"

Andries looked at the group, turning ideas over in his mind. Adriana thought he expected some contribution from her.

"Well, couldn't you . . . couldn't you just fire these cannons as they go by?" she finally brought out timidly, indicating the old guns on the wall.

A roaring horse laugh was all she got from the boys. Andries even tapped his forehead to show that he'd never let such an outlandish idea out of *his* brain.

"They're left over from the eighteenth century—from the days of the East India Company!" Machiel informed her.

"At least if they were machine guns!" Andries added.

"How's Adriana supposed to know about the East India Company!" Tannie demanded, trying to save her friend. "They never came to Schouwen, isn't that so, Adriana?"

"Say, Wolfert," Andries began again. "How . . ."

Yes, how? Wolfert didn't know, but he would never have admitted it. "Now look, you fishermen," he said craftily. "I don't know boats as well as you do." The fishing boys thought until their brains were about to burst.

Suddenly Andries yelled, "I've got it!" This time the others could see by his expression that it was true. They jumped off the wall on which they had been sitting and expectantly listened to Andries, who stood in the center of their little circle.

"We're each going to make sure we're on board one of the cutters the night before March thirtieth. Well, maybe we'll do it the same afternoon. Okay? And then each of us'll take a spark plug out of the engine of the ship he's on. You'll never get a ship to move without spark plugs!"

The excitement that met his plan was so overwhelming that Andries started to wave his arms angrily. "Shh! You don't have to let everybody in Veere know about it!"

"What a plot! It's wonderful!" Tannie said, hugely impressed. She hadn't any idea what spark plugs were, but she'd find out soon enough.

"Let's go and have a look right now!" Wolfert bounded up, itching for action. He was all set to run off to the ships immediately, but Andries and Machiel stopped him.

"*We* don't need to," Andries said haughtily.

"Oh, well, maybe not," Wolfert agreed. "But I've never even seen the insides of a boat."

"Well, you can't right now." Machiel was firm. "And anyway do you have to let out the plan so soon?" He surprised himself with his angry tone.

It's only a game for Wolfert, Machiel thought rather bitterly. He doesn't have to leave. Dam or no dam, his father's farm will still be here. But we . . . He thought of the day the ships really would be sailing out for the last time—his father's ship, the *Ve 20,* along with the others. He pictured his father and the men swarming busily in the harbor, and he recalled Gilles's sober pronouncement: "Madness, sheer madness!" Even as he had these thoughts, he wondered why he couldn't get all excited about it like Andries.

"Why don't you say anything?" Andries demanded. "You *are* going along with it, aren't you?" He looked sharply at his friend.

"Of course," Machiel growled in reply.

Was he going to go along with it? Certainly he was! And

yet he really didn't want to. How could you want to and not want to do something at the same time?

"Then it's all set. And we'll think of something to do to the men who are working on the dam too!" Andries promised darkly. "Once you've begun, you know . . . Later on . . ."

All at once a gruff voice behind them barked out: "Well aren't you all in a great big huddle! Planning to go along to The Hague tomorrow?"

Starting guiltily, the children looked around.

7
THE FATHERS
GO TO THE HAGUE

OLD Arjaan, who manned the lifeboat, stood behind them, a bag of crayfish for the hotel slung over his shoulder.

"Secret meeting?" he asked jokingly. But the children saw the curiosity gleaming in his light blue eyes. Tannie nudged Machiel so he wouldn't give them away. If Arjaan knew your plans you might just as well shout them from the Town Hall Tower. Machiel's only answer was to turn his eyes all the way up and then down again toward Tannie, as if to say, "Do you think I'm out of my mind!" Tannie giggled at Adriana.

Andries, too, had been looking at the others significantly. Well, finally the grownups were coming up with a scheme too. "It's about time!" he muttered softly. It wouldn't do to have Arjaan asking about their plans, so Andries quickly asked, "Who's going to The Hague, Arjaan?" Andries knew the old fisherman would jump at the opportunity to tell his news. He loved collecting bits of information and broadcasting them.

The diversion worked. Arjaan squinted craftily so that even more wrinkles appeared in his face, and looked mysteriously over the children's heads. "Tomorrow," he said vaguely. "The Fishermen's Council."

"Oh?" "Who?" "And what are *they* going to do?" Questions came flying at Arjaan from all sides, and the old man thoroughly enjoyed the stir he had caused.

"All of them. All the members of the Fishermen's Council, that's who," he informed them, shrugging his shoulders. He looked at Machiel for an instant, as if to say, "Your father too." "They've planned it for a long time, and now a message has come to the Town Hall that the Prime Minister will see them. He's not free every day, you know."

"I don't know anything about it," Wolfert remarked shortly.

"That's as it ought to be. Are *you* a Councilman?" Tannie demanded.

"They're going to ask if a sluice gate can't be put in," Arjaan said.

"But it's all settled," Wolfert snorted with great self-confidence. "They've been talking about it long enough in the Council. My father says the Burgomaster says they're going to have a lock out."

"So?" Machiel raised his eyebrows.

"So that means we're going to get a sluice gate to lock out the sea."

"Oh, silly! You don't know what you're talking about!"

"Don't you dare try to tell me . . ." Wolfert shouted, ready for another fight.

Suddenly Old Arjaan screamed at them. "Quit it! Haven't you had enough of your eternal fighting? Don't you have anything else on your minds? Haven't we all had enough madness?"

Startled, they held their tongues, and Gilles's fierce comment, "Madness!" came back to Machiel. Arjaan was furious now and deadly serious. He talked almost to himself as he bound string around his sack.

"All things come in threes. First they chased us out of Arnemuiden. No, you wouldn't know anything about that—you're too young. But the boats can't sail from Arnemuiden any more, they have to sail from Veere. Now they're chasing us out of Veere. What about Colijnsplaat? Before ten years have passed it'll be shut up tight too. Then the fishermen will have to pull up stakes again. And then the movie makers can have another field day and let the whole country in on it."

The children listened uncomfortably. They never knew quite what to do when an adult got really upset. At the words "movie makers" they pricked up their ears and looked at each other significantly. But when Arjaan mentioned ten years, they sighed with relief. Ten years! A whole eternity, they thought.

"Just wait and see, Arjaan," Andries said brusquely. He was just about to proclaim that they—he and his friends—were going to do something about the film, but the old man was no longer listening. He was off in his own thoughts, not even seeing the children standing before him.

"That Delta Plan—it's a big thing. And what is a fisherman? Nothing. Absolutely nothing. And that's why nothing will come of the visit to The Hague."

Only Machiel, standing closest to Arjaan, saw the expression on the old man's face. He cleared his throat.

"Maybe they *will* . . ." He had been about to say that the Fishermen's Council might still get the sluice gate they were fighting for. But Arjaan had picked up his sack.

"Let me by," he said. "I'm off to the Tower with my crayfish. Dainty little tidbits for the tourists." His voice was mocking again.

He left, walking slowly, and the children still stood in the same little circle. But their previous mood of high excitement was gone, like a balloon deflated with a pinprick. They looked at each other, bewildered.

"It's always you," Andries growled at Wolfert. "You're always the one that starts the trouble. First with the teacher, and now you pick a fight with Arjaan. He didn't even look back at us."

"All things come in threes, he said," Joris remarked thoughtfully. "I wonder . . . ?"

But Wolfert protested furiously: "I never pick a fight. It wasn't my fault. And who thought up The Plan? And who . . . you were the one . . ."

"Oh, stop it," Machiel begged. "It wasn't anyone's fault. I mean . . . well . . . that's just the way it is." Miserably, he hunched his shoulders, and his eyes shifted toward the west. He looked at the ships standing in neat rows. They were all scrubbed down and fresh, ready to sail out. Two deck hands sat on the *Arn 14,* eating some bread and butter. Behind the little group of children, there was the sound of wooden shoes hitting the cobblestones and every now and then they could hear the tinkle of Mrs. Hubregse's doorbell. Some fishing boys went on deck with provisions—all the others had gone home already. Machiel watched as though he had never seen the scene before.

"Pathetic, an old man like that," Tannie said. "It's the second time for him."

The boys muttered; they never used words like "pathetic." Gruffly, Andries said, "Well, at least it ought to be clear to everyone now that a movie mustn't be allowed. We're not monkeys in a zoo!"

The reference to monkeys relieved their mood a little, and some of them even smiled, but Andries looked as stern as ever. He even looked older, Machiel reflected, as though what happened in Veere was a matter of personal interest to him, not just to the grownups. And after all, wasn't it their personal concern? "We will carry out The Plan," he pronounced solemnly.

"That's what I say too!" Joris piped up. He looked a bit surprised at his own courage, but when Tannie shot him an approving glance he added, "There's nothing wrong with it, is there?" At least they weren't talking about dynamite now.

A shout came from the distance, down by the hotel.

"Quiet, someone's calling," Adriana said. The west wind brought old Arjaan's voice to them, vague and indistinct: ". . . your teacher . . . going to The Hague too." They saw him wave; then he disappeared behind the Campveerse Tower.

The children's eyes sparkled. Their teacher going too? But of course—it made sense! Where would you find a stronger partisan of Veere? And besides . . .

Wolfert picked up the unspoken thought. "What luck!" he sighed gratefully. The others jumped with delight, and all of them thought feverishly of what they would do with the unexpected holiday.

"Of course that business of The Hague won't help a bit," Machiel remarked. "But at least . . ." Before he even had a chance to finish, Andries jabbed him excitedly in the ribs, so hard they almost cracked.

"Say, Machiel! Couldn't we go along on the ship? Then we could . . ."

Andries had been about to say that it would be a great chance to rehearse their planned sabotage. But his friend, rubbing his ribs, shook his dark head so definitely that Andries stopped before he had finished.

"Out of the question," said Machiel. "I'm never allowed to go along when Father isn't around. I don't even have to ask."

"Well of course I can understand that," Andries admitted. "But . . ." They all had the same thing on their minds. Wasn't there anything else they could start doing about The Plan?

"Listen," Machiel began. "We've decided to carry it out. And Andries and I will work something out before the deadline. After all, it's a simple plan."

"Well, all right," Andries said. "But what about tomorrow? Because if I stay home I'll have to help with the nets. And chop wood." The others nodded sympathetically. They all had the same problem.

"Suppose we all go to the construction site," Machiel suggested, trying to sound casual. But he looked eagerly at the faces before him, especially at Andries, who frowned. They had never been there, because they knew instinctively that their fathers would rather they did not go. Every day the fishermen sailed past the swarms of men working on the dam, past the seven caissons. They certainly didn't want to come to blows with these men, even though every once in a while someone might make a sarcastic remark. After all, their fathers weren't schoolboys any more. But to go and look around of their own free wills? No. The children understood without ever having to be told, and so they thought the suggestion over carefully.

"After all, it's a perfectly ordinary thing to do," Tannie said, after a pause.

"They never actually *said* we couldn't go," Andries added.

"There are signs all over the place: *No Admittance*," Wolfert said. "My father . . ."

"Oh, why doesn't your precious father go to The Hague tomorrow too!" Machiel snapped, and the others glowered at Wolfert.

"No Admittance!" Andries sneered. "As if we'd let that stop us!"

"I didn't say it was going to stop us!" Wolfert answered, backtracking quickly. If he didn't watch out they wouldn't let him come along tomorrow. And then he'd have to stake beets in the fields. No, he'd much rather . . .

"Well, we've got to do *something* with a free day like that," Machiel remarked. "And we've never been there. At least . . ." He was about to say that he had wandered over in that direction before, but he quickly swallowed his words. After all, it was nobody's business.

Andries looked at his friend carefully. Why was he so eager to go to the construction site? His father certainly wouldn't take very kindly to the idea. But Machiel's dark face showed nothing.

"Hmm. Well, maybe it is a good idea," Andries admitted.

"Hurray!" Tannie clapped her hands in delight and dealt out playful jabs right and left. "And maybe we'll find something there to sabotage too!"

She looked around as if she were ready to take on the whole world, and Machiel broke into a rare grin. But Tannie was in such a good mood she wasn't paying any attention to that. A whole day free! And spending it with the gang! That was really something else!

"We'll take some bread along!" she said.

"Oh, come on! It's not a picnic!" Wolfert objected.

"We'll see," Andries said. He looked about. "Say, let's race to the windmill." He pointed to the high green wall in the distance. A moment later the little troop dashed along the quay, shrieking happily. Wolfert slipped on a shrimp, fell down and then ran on, hitching his trousers up as he went. Machiel and Andries were ahead, with Tannie right behind them. Way back Joris panted along, and Adriana was almost out of sight behind them all. When they had reached the water which reflected the white windmill and its sweeping sails, Andries yelled, "Till tomorrow, then! And think about The Plan! Not a word to anyone. The password is 'shrimp'!"

Laughing at that parting remark, the children spread out to various parts of the little town. Silence had descended over the quay with its boats. The water splashed up, and the wind blew over the land from the sea.

Toward six Machiel flew over the cobblestones of the quay on his bicycle. It was later than he had thought. He had promised to bring Dingenis some new rope, and he still had to pick up the milk and porridge. That was his chore, and he was very proud that neither his father nor his brother ever had to check the provisions on board.

Still panting from his swift ride against the wind, he came into Mrs. Hubregse's little store. Just in time. Father and Dingenis would never know that he had ridden over just to take a quick look at the caissons and see how far they had got. He had certainly not expected to meet the new boy there. The latter had called him by name as he rode past. No more than that. But Machiel, who had been too taken aback to say more than "Hi!" had felt cheered by it. He thought about it, standing on the threshold of the little store, until suddenly he heard the carillon above his head. Six o'clock!

He flew into the store with such vigor that a couple of fisher-

men who were standing around turned toward him. They said
nothing, but that left Mrs. Hubregse all the more to say.

"Hey! Can't you do that a bit more calmly? You scare
people half to death!"

"I . . . I had to . . ." Machiel stuttered. He got the feeling
they were all watching him. His Uncle Meindert's mate hoisted
a heavy sea bag, bottles sticking bulkily out of it, onto one
shoulder. Over the other he said:

"Well, you know a man can be in a hurry once in his life!"
The others grinned.

"Better get a move on," Machiel thought. But a man from
Arnemuiden needed six lengths of maintop rope, and the box
which usually contained it was empty. Why not take the kind
with the bolts on it? That would be the next best thing. No,
that wouldn't quite do, and Mrs. Hubregse had to shuffle back
again. Sighing, Machiel looked after her.

When he finally did get his order in, she was surprised.
"But Dingenis came for it long ago—at least half an hour ago.
He said they had to have it on board by seven, you know."

"Okay," Machiel replied, and left the store. Home again,
he shoved open the door which led from the little back street
into the garden and leaned his bicycle against a buttress in the
wall. He dashed through the garden and into the kitchen,
whistling loudly, but his father was not there. Only Moei
Katrina shuffled through from the living room into the kitchen
on her flapping slippers. She hardly paid any attention to
Machiel except to mutter as she passed him:

"They're going to The Hague. To see the Queen!"

Dingenis stood by the window reading a newspaper. He
frowned at Machiel.

"Isn't Father back yet?" Machiel asked. He tried to act as
usual. And why shouldn't he? Everything was just as it was

any other evening, except for the fact that he had managed to forget the porridge. And also Allard had said hello to him. What had *he* been doing prowling around there? All at once Machiel's thoughts were so far away that Dingenis noticed the unusual silence.

"Now just sit down somewhere or go away," he said, a bit crossly.

"The bottles . . ." Machiel began. Now he'd let it out after all! That's the way it always went. Well, he had no choice— he'd just have to go on. "Mrs. Hubregse said you'd already been to pick them up."

Dingenis turned to face his brother. He even took his cigarette out of his mouth. "Of course I picked them up. I saw you ride off and I knew you wouldn't get back in time from *there*. And Father has to leave tomorrow. So . . ."

"But that's silly!" Machiel protested. But Dingenis didn't want to go into the matter.

"I don't care what you do after school hours," Dingenis said. His eyes looked right into Machiel's face, eyes like his father's, only much fiercer. "But I don't want you playing up to any of those people with the Waterworks Authority."

"I . . ." Machiel began. Had Dingenis seen him? What else could it have been? "I . . ."

"I'm not saying those people don't have to be there," Dingenis continued undisturbed, "but they'll never get onto *my* ship, I'll tell you that!" His voice sounded threatening. "And I'm not going to quit working just because of them!" He turned and stalked out of the room.

Machiel scolded himself furiously; he never could think up a good answer on time. "Play up!" All he'd said was "Hi!" How silly could the whole thing get?

Angrily he tore open the paper that Dingenis had left, but then he let it fall again. Newspapers. What good were newspapers! Thoroughly dissatisfied, he opened the door to the front room and only then did he see that his father was sitting there with the other members of the Fishermen's Council. It was too late for him to turn back, so he opened his mouth to apologize if necessary. But no one had noticed him, and Machiel remained standing. Smoke hung in the room, and the figures of his father and his Uncle Meindert looked like bluish ghosts, sitting at the table. Even Old Arjaan was there. Sentences flew through the room:

"Everyone knows that you're completely open and exposed in Colijn. They have to do something to protect the harbor. The way it is now, all you need is a strong wind blowing from that corner. What do you get then, my friend? A swell, and not just a little one. The ships will pitch and roll." That was Andries's father, Skipper Domisse.

"But we'll be able to manage," Skipper Cevaal replied. As though hearing his father's voice for the first time, Machiel noticed how it had changed. It was more thoughtful, yes, but also warmer and less sharp than ever before.

"Be able to manage!" Skipper Domisse shouted. It was no wonder that he, Machiel, was so different from Andries. Andries was hot-tempered, sharp, quick with his words. He was sluggish, not so fast. Machiel looked on curiously, forgetting the discussion was supposed to be private.

"Be able to manage," Skipper Domisse repeated scornfully. "Your hawsers will break like string. And just wait and see what your old tub will look like when it's been rammed by a couple of others!"

"Well, you'll be in Colijn too," Skipper Cevaal said.

Others added remarks, but it was always Skipper Domisse who spoke loudest and most bitterly.

"And what about Saturdays and Sundays? When we all go back to Veere or Arnemuiden to be with our families? Who'll take care of your boat then, when there's a wild nor'easter? It'll break adrift, and nobody over there will give a hang!" By "over there" Machiel knew his uncle meant The Hague. He heard a mutter of agreement, but his father's voice sounded cool and resolute:

"If you live there you will be able to look after your boat. And you know as well as I do, Meindert, that it will have to come to that."

"Never! As long as I live!" Skipper Domisse shouted. "I'm staying in Veere, I tell you, and that's final!"

"They haven't even built a single house there yet," a heated voice cried. Machiel stuck his head further into the room to see who it was, but now his father noticed him. Quickly Machiel pulled his head back. Too late.

"Hey, Machiel! Run and tell your uncle that we'll pick him up at a quarter to seven." But a new argument was now brewing over in the corner, and Machiel didn't move.

"Have you seen the bollards over there? No one will ever be able to moor properly."

"How are you going to get to the fishing grounds from there in those boats? You'll have to put in a completely different engine."

"Then we'll put one in," Machiel heard his father say. "It's high time the fleet was modernized anyway. But we're not discussing that now."

"And who will pay for that? You don't seem to care about anything! Nothing bothers you! And we don't even know anything for sure about government compensation."

"Of course I care about that, Meindert," Machiel's father said quietly. But now his voice had a warning note in it which made Machiel draw back. If his Uncle Meindert didn't take the hint . . .

"I told you to take a message to Uncle Bouterse," Skipper Cevaal said unexpectedly. "Get going."

He had spoken no louder than before, but that "get going" was definite, and Machiel closed the door tightly behind him. He felt uneasy.

Skipper Bouterse stood grinning down at Machiel before he fully realized he was standing on the threshold and had already rung the bell.

"Has the dam addled your brain too?" his uncle asked teasingly. "Don't worry about it before the time comes. You'll see what the Prime Minister will do for us tomorrow."

Machiel hunched his shoulders. Well, let Uncle Bouterse think that if he wanted to. He'd stick to their own Plan. At least *their* Plan would bring results!

"Father says they'll pick you up at a quarter to seven tomorrow morning," he said.

"Pick up whom for what at a quarter to seven tomorrow?" Skipper Bouterse pretended innocence, but Machiel was already down the step and didn't hear him.

"It's a good thing they're not taking you along," his uncle yelled after him peevishly.

"Huh! Wouldn't want to go anyhow!" Machiel replied over his shoulder. He thought over The Plan again as he walked home. Yes, it would have to be carried out. Then at least you'd have the feeling you were doing something for your father and the other fishermen, even if they didn't like The Plan. He'd explain it all to them later on, when everything had gone off according to schedule. Wouldn't it be wonderful to see that movie maker's face when not one of the ships could move! And tomorrow, over there by the caissons . . .

He was still awake late at night. His aunt had scolded him because he hadn't come right in to eat. She meant no harm, she just had to complain all the time. Then she had set a plate with four thick slices of bread and butter before him. Sjakie was in bed already, and Machiel hadn't spoken to Dingenis again before he left on board the ship.

When the fishermen left their homes at two o'clock, Machiel raised his head, listening. He often awoke at this hour of the night.

His father was not going along tonight. Would they get a sluice gate after all? Machiel wondered. "A sluice gate, with fate . . ." No, that wasn't the way their slogan went.

A dam like that wasn't a simple matter at all, he thought. What a mass of boats and cranes and barges there were out there. Go and see tomorrow after all. They used nylon mattresses to rest the caissons on, Mr. Risseeuw had once said. Were they really strong enough? Machiel had heard of altogether different mattresses, made out of willows.

Outside, two pairs of wooden shoes still clattered. The bollards couldn't be used in Colijnsplaat. You couldn't moor solidly alongside the quay as you could here; you had to tie up at right angles to it, in rows next to one another. And the engines . . .

Allard's father was an engineer. What did a man like that actually do? The last footsteps went past, and for a time the noise died down. The first engine started up, growling. A couple of others roared off. While the fishing vessels sailed out past the Veere Gap, Machiel slept.

8
A VISIT
TO THE CAISSONS

THEY pedaled out of Veere and along Fort The Hague Road like runners at the starting gun.

"Let's go!" Andries yelled. "Don't let our mothers catch us —or Machiel's aunt—or they'll stick us with the chores! Hey, watch it, you dope!" he yelled at Joris, who was thinking of all the shoes he should have delivered that morning.

"Come on!" Tannie shouted.

"It's really great—a morning like this," Joris said as he pedaled his bicycle.

"Huh? What did you say?" Tannie started and looked at the boy's good-natured, shy face.

Tannie was riding next to him, and Joris felt ten feet tall. "It's crazy—school day after day," he said daringly.

"Taaaaaneeeee!" Adriana's voice shrilled. Tannie braked hard.

"Come with us! We're going out!" she yelled. She knew Machiel and Andries wouldn't like having another girl along, but that was just too bad. She slackened speed and waited for her friend to bring up the rear of the little procession.

Allard van Beusekom wandered about, scuffing up the clay between the Vrouwen polder and Veere. His father had left for the construction shacks on the beach early in the morning, long before the boy was awake. Allard was at loose ends this holiday. What should he do with all the time hanging heavy on his hands?

"Why don't you take a ride through Veere? It's a very lovely little town," his mother had suggested. "Or why don't you go and look at the caissons? There's always something to watch there."

"I'll see," he answered. It wasn't very pleasant around here for his mother, and he certainly didn't want to burden her with what he thought of Veere. Lovely little town. Nothing but a handful of houses. I'd have to be crazy to go over there, he thought. Besides, he'd run the risk of bumping into that gang from school. Later, when he got to know a few of the boys, that might not be so bad, but right now he didn't want to see them. What else was there to do? There were the caissons, of course, but he had seen them so many times.

He shielded his eyes against the bright sun shining on the sea and looked toward the construction site. He could go over there and look around, after all. They were finishing the last caisson now, his father had said yesterday. But just let them catch you around there. They always chased children away, all except Mr. Naerebouts, the overseer; he was nice. He had once let Allard tighten some screws. "Then you'll be able to say you actually worked on the famous caissons," he had said. Finally Allard decided that he would go to the construction site.

Suddenly he caught sight of the little group from Veere. They've come to give me a rough time, he assumed immediately. But they've got another thought coming. Quickly he looked about for a good hiding place. He remembered that Indians about to be attacked always looked for good cover from which to launch a counterattack.

He searched the rolling dunes and the glistening water until his eyes lit on a huge mountain of basalt blocks to his left. In a flash, Allard reached the top: he had a clear view all around and could keep the gang in sight. He teetered for a moment, then bent to scoop up some rocks. Not too big, but after all, you could never tell what the others were planning to do. He was so caught up with collecting ammunition that he started at the rattle of an old bicycle and the sound of voices. They were close.

Hurriedly he pushed up his sleeves. He planted his feet far apart and gripped a piece of basalt firmly in his right hand. With his left hand he held onto a huge boulder and peeped out from behind. He could hear the leaders wheezing loudly, fat Wolfert puffing louder than any of the others. Had they seen him? Allard listened carefully for the sound of brakes. Here they came! Quickly he ducked; then he looked out, stealthy as a cat, following their movements. That was Tannie's shrill voice, and the loud one must be Andries. Now he'd pop up suddenly on the other side with his rock, and then . . .

But when he came out of his hiding place, all he could see were Adriana's and Tannie's backs. Allard could barely make out Machiel's blue cap. His hand fell slackly to his side, and the stone plopped onto the basalt. They hadn't even seen him.

"There they are, boys!"
Andries Domisse's voice carried above the roar of the wind.

"Now what, Machieltje? Shall we take them home with us?"

Machiel had laid his bike on the ground and stood leaning against the red and white barrier separating the construction area from the road, staring silently at the seven structures. From Veere they had often seen the huge caissons taking shape on the horizon. One day they were hazy and mysterious, another day sharply outlined. They were familiar sights, but now that the children were standing so close to them they were much more deeply impressed than they would have cared to admit. Terrifyingly high, thick and massive, the concrete giants seemed to stare down at them.

Machiel and Andries stood before them, trying to look nonchalant. They tilted their heads back, spread their legs apart and whistled tunelessly between their teeth. Behind them Wolfert fussed with his new bicycle, the girls watching silently. The saddle was too high, and he tugged at the stand, his face red.

"How high would you guess?" Andries asked Machiel.

"Too high for your short legs, in any case," Tannie said, watching her brother.

"What?" cried Andries. "Oh, you . . ."

"Well, at least about sixty feet," Machiel judged. "Maybe ninety. Hey, look up there, on top!"

High up on the seventh caisson figures swarmed against the clouds, busy workmen in boots and overalls. A huge crane on rails rode past the seven giants, handing materials down with its iron claws. From all sides the noise echoed and re-echoed. Now and then a bluish flame would shoot eerily through the whole framework of the caisson. The puny figures moved and bent, working. They were small, but seemed important because they were allowed to be up there.

"Come closer with me," Machiel said suddenly, stooping under the barrier.

"That's not allowed," Joris objected, pointing to a sign: *No Admittance to Unauthorized Persons.*

"Then you stay with the little girlies," Andries shot back. His sharp brown eyes glided over the faces of Tannie and Adriana and then rested on Wolfert.

"Well, Councilman. Coming along? *You're* certainly authorized!"

"Well now, that is . . ." Wolfert stuttered. He didn't quite know whether to be flattered or not when Andries called him Councilman. And what about his bicycle—his brand new bicycle? Suppose he got caught? He looked about quite flustered. Wait—behind that pile of rocks! He wheeled the bike over quickly and, panting, caught up with the others who had already ducked under the barrier. Even Joris tagged along.

"If we keep to the right a bit," Andries whispered, "they won't see us. There's only a handful of them."

It was true. Where only a few weeks before hundreds of men had been busy day and night, only fifteen figures now stood out against the sky. If you stood right beneath the first caisson you couldn't even see them any more.

More threatening than ever, the tremendous white walls loomed above the children. Sea gulls rose up screaming. Machiel shivered. Andries called out something, but he didn't even hear. People in Veere talked of the caissons as if they were concrete tanks which you could just sink into the sea. Uncle Meindert even called them "coffins." But these mighty structures were more like full-scale factories—seven of them next to one another. Just look at all the latticework, Machiel exclaimed to himself. And all the steps. How did those sliding gratings work? Just think—the entire immense structure would disappear into the sea!

"Funny to think of all that just being plopped into the water." Tannie echoed Machiel's thought.

"I was thinking the same thing," he said, and Tannie colored with pleasure. But soon Machiel and Andries, ignoring Tannie altogether, were busily discussing the height of the caissons from the ground, the number of steps on the sides, the name of the topmost piece—on which the men were working—what it was for and how the sliding grates worked. Their voices got louder and more earnest:

". . . first they dug this long ditch over here. That's where they're building all seven of them, one after the other so the crane can pass along them in a straight line. You didn't think that huge thing could go in circles, did you?" Machiel's voice rang excitedly through the cold air. "Well, then. See, they keep the concrete mixer over there, on the other side; I'll show you later. Then all they have to do is stuff each caisson full of concrete!"

"Seems you know all about it," Andries remarked a bit peevishly. "How do they get those monster things into the sea? I still don't like the looks of them."

Machiel paid no attention to his friend's negative tone. His forehead furrowed in concentration, he looked at the narrow dike which ran parallel to the shore, all the way out to the dam. Somehow the caissons, which were being constructed in drydock, would have to be brought across the dike up to the dam.

"You must think they're on wheels and they'll just bump right over the dike," Andries said mockingly.

"Not bump right over. They . . . well, they'll find something," Machiel finished positively. He didn't know the answer to that question either, but he'd find out. What fantastic things those caissons were! And Allard's father had something to do with them.

But the girls had seen all they cared to see of the caissons. And besides, they thought, as soon as the boys saw anything that could be driven or moved, anything being constructed or demolished, they didn't pay any attention to you any more.

"You know, I'm a bit disappointed," Tannie said, addressing the remark to Machiel. He did not respond.

A sudden mischievous thought occurred to her: "Would you dare climb up?" she challenged.

Machiel and Andries turned around, amazed.

"Well, it's possible, you know," Tannie added defensively.

"Everything's possible . . ." Andries began.

"Yes, yes! Come on, boys, let's go!" Wolfert cried excitedly. "Want to bet? Want to bet you can make it?"

"You first!" Adriana cut in all at once; she was almost frightened at her own courage. But Wolfert fell back immediately.

"Well, I mean . . . well, I have to keep an eye on my bike, you know. If it weren't for that, of course . . ." He saw the others' looks and added quickly, "But I'll bet a *kwartje* you two wouldn't do it!"

Tannie clutched her hands in excitement and Machiel and Andries looked at one another, then at Wolfert, then at the gigantic caissons looming over them. Nonchalantly, Wolfert played with a *kwartje,* holding it temptingly in front of the boys.

"I don't need your old *kwartje,*" Andries snapped.

"You don't dare. You're scared you'll fall," Wolfert taunted.

"Fall!" Andries yelled, and Machiel laughed scornfully. "Well, you can sure tell *you've* never been on a ship at night. Fall off something that's standing still! Even a shrimp has more sense than you do!"

"Okay. You going up or not?"

Andries looked over the row of caissons carefully.

"I bet I'm up there before the next thirty minutes are past," he said.

"Oh no!" Adriana screamed, and even Tannie tried to stop them. "It was only a joke, Andries. Don't be crazy. No one can climb that!"

"Nonsense," the boy answered. "*Those* fellows got up there. Machiel, you coming?"

Machiel looked up again, just once.

"Keep watch," he commanded. "We'll start over here. This caisson was the first one ready, so they won't come back to it for a while." Obediently, the girls posted themselves on both sides of the caisson. Wolfert carefully surveyed the terrain and chose a heap of clay sticking out above the surrounding flat land. There he stood, like a field marshal overseeing his troops.

"Get off there, you idiot!" Andries snarled. "They'll be able to see us from ten miles away if you stand there like that. Get down in the grass. That's the way!" he called. The two climbers took a deep breath, cleared their throats, and gripped the iron hand holds leading to the very top of the sheer walls.

"Easy as pie," Andries whispered. "If you just . . ."

Machiel held up his hand and listened intently.

"What is it?" Andries hissed.

"I thought I heard something . . ."

"You can always hear something around here. The wind . . . and the sea." Andries didn't mention that he could also hear his heart knocking loudly against his ribs. What if they got to the top of the caissons and those guys came along? He saw that Machiel had the same thought.

You can't jump off, Andries thought. Shh! What was that? They looked back for a moment, but all they could see was the girls' arms waving against the gray sky like little sticks.

"That's right! First they egg you on. Then they get cold feet," Andries grumbled. "But we're going up anyway. You know we should have brought the football team flag up with us—we could have planted it up there. Wouldn't you just love to see those people's faces!"

"My handkerchief is red. Maybe we could use that," Machiel said.

He was already several dozen feet up. He saw the sea and behind him the broad, flat polders of Walcheren. He smelled the wind, just like on the ship. And he felt marvelously proud, even though he was afraid. He grasped the hand holds firmly, one above the other, and his feet groped beneath him. "Never let go with more than one hand or foot when you're climbing," Mr. Risseeuw had told them.

"He's actually in The Hague," Machiel muttered. "And our fathers along with him."

"Say something?" Andries asked, panting beneath him.

"No—just thought—wouldn't the Prime Minister stare if he saw us up here now?"

But there was no answer, and when Machiel looked around carefully, he saw his friend in full retreat, getting down as fast as he could. At the same moment a savage bark shattered the silence. A huge dog, his jaws open and snarling, came dashing up and ran back and forth in front of the caissons, less than a hundred feet from them.

Machiel screamed and scrambled down as fast as he could, hardly looking where he was putting his feet. Two dull thuds on the sand as he landed, and he and Andries dashed madly off, a hoarse voice screaming after them. A man ran alongside the bottom of the caissons, waving furiously in the distance.

The children scrambled madly under the barrier and down the road. They grabbed their bicycles, knocking heads together in their hurry and flung themselves on their seats. The barking got weaker and fainter until they left it behind completely.

They were almost at Veere before they dared stop. They heard each other's panting breath and looked at one another. Machiel and Andries were scowling because everyone had seen their shameful flight, and the others kicked themselves for not keeping a better lookout.

"Well, so much for that," Andries said in a strangled voice.

"Next time you get any bright ideas, keep them to yourself, you hear?" Machiel threatened, giving Wolfert a dirty look.

"That guy's dog . . . looked more like a tiger!" said Joris hoarsely. But the girls looked at the two heroes in such embarrassment that Machiel coughed and tried to pretend he didn't care. He pulled out his red handkerchief with white polka dots and grimly mopped his streaming face. Andries stared at the red cloth; just think—he'd wanted to plant that at the very top of the caisson. He could sink through the ground with shame. And all because of a dog!

"Well *I* think you were just great anyway! You looked just like—like mountain climbers in the movies. Didn't they, Tannie?" Adriana piped up bravely, and Tannie nodded heartily. She didn't dare say too much yet; after all, she had cooked up the whole plan.

"Did we really look that way?" Andries asked. "Hm." He passed his hand through his soaking hair and looked at Machiel.

"Oh, well," he remarked. After all, things didn't always go right for the boys in the books he read. He made a sweeping gesture, as if to say the circumstances were quite beyond anyone's control. The others sighed with relief.

"How about a break?" Machiel suggested, pointing to an old rowboat pulled up on the shore.

"I've got some chocolate," Tannie remembered. Nervously she rummaged in all her pockets, finally fishing a broken and crumpled bar out of the bottom of the very last one she tried. They sat down in the old boat, munching silently. Tannie stole a glance at Machiel. Had he noticed she'd given him two pieces and kept none for herself? But Machiel was staring back in the direction of the caissons.

"Someone's coming," he said. Joris shot straight up, but Andries pulled him down hard. He practically choked on his chocolate.

"Sit down, you dope. It's a policeman, and they're always suspicious anyway. If you look scared he'll think we've done something. Act casual."

"Act casual! Act casual! *You* try!" Joris exploded. He bounded up again.

"Come on, Joris! Look at me! That's it!" And Tannie deadpanned so smoothly the others suddenly burst into roars of laughter. When the policeman rode by, they were lying on their backs on top of each other in the rowboat, shrieking with laughter.

The policeman slowed down and scowled at the group.

"I'm warning you!" he threatened.

Joris giggled faintly at the bottom of the heap. "The watch-word is 'shrimp'!"

"We're . . . we're . . . ooh!" Tannie burst out helplessly.

The man looked around grimly once again and rode on, so slowly that his wheels wobbled.

"He's going to fall," Tannie said hopefully.

"Oh, grownups!" Machiel burst out. "I've heard it at least a hundred times! They never have anything better to say than 'I'm warning you!' or 'Watch out!' or 'Take care!' "

"My mother says that all the time," Adriana agreed.

"But what are we supposed to watch out *for?*" Tannie asked indignantly. "They never tell us that. And they always think we're going to do something wrong!"

Andries grinned. "Well, just now . . ." he said.

He jerked at the battered straps in the oar-locks. "Hey, skipper! Let's go!" he called. "Hey! where's your cap?"

With a shock, Machiel felt his head. His cap wasn't there.

"You had it while you were climbing," Tannie reassured him. Scornfully, her brother looked at her.

"Well, you're really up on things!"

"Oh, shut your trap!" Machiel snapped, angry at losing his cap and even angrier that he'd let his annoyance show. Rest-lessly he looked around the boat, in the sand, down the road. Nothing.

"What do you need that thing on your head for, anyway!" Wolfert remarked petulantly.

"Mind your own business," Machiel shot back.

"Now, now, boys," Tannie pleaded, and Adriana added, "What do you care about an old cap!"

Machiel simply looked at her. How could he tell her he *did* care, and that his cap wasn't just any old cap—that it had something to do with what he wanted to be; that he'd worn it that night long ago on the ship, when his mother had stood waiting on the quay for him. Without his cap he felt naked. And to go and lose it here, of all places!

"Must have flown off," he said as carelessly as he could. "I'll catch up with you. Don't wait for me." He jumped out of the boat and grabbed his bicycle.

Allard van Beusekom saw him coming, and this time he didn't hide behind a basalt mountain. He waited till Machiel was close, and then he said loudly:

"Didn't like that, did you?" Machiel started at the unexpected voice slicing through his thoughts.

"What?" he asked, more sharply than he had meant to. He held his bike still with the tip of one shoe.

"Being chased off the caisson," Allard answered, looking straight at Machiel.

"Oh, that." Who else had seen him, Machiel wondered, and Allard seemed to guess his thought:

"Must have figured I didn't see you!"

Machiel felt for the visor of his cap, trying to think of an answer. But his cap was gone, and he looked around uneasily.

"What were you trying to do?"

"Did you sic that fellow with the dog on us?" Machiel countered, but Allard shrugged his shoulders so scornfully that Machiel was embarrassed to have asked.

"The gamekeeper from the Vrouwen polder!" Allard exclaimed. "All he has to do is show his face and the brave Veere fishermen run!"

Machiel flushed with shame and fury. A gamekeeper! Good thing Andries wasn't here.

"What *are* you doing here?" Allard repeated, in a rather unfriendly tone.

"Well now, in case you didn't know, Fort The Hague Road is a public road—anyone can walk along it."

Now it was Allard's turn to color at Machiel's sarcasm.

"You people won't let me on your ships, though, will you?" There was something in his voice that suddenly touched Machiel, and he looked searchingly at the other boy. In a flash he understood more of Allard's loneliness and resentment than he could ever have told Allard.

"*I* never said that," Machiel said simply.

Allard looked at him; he saw a dark face with greenish-gray eyes that reminded him of the sea, and thick, black hair which he hadn't noticed so much before. Suddenly he realized that Machiel didn't have his cap on. What was he saying? "*I* never said that!" It was true. It was that miserable Wolfert who had said it. But didn't that come to the same thing? They had chased him away and laughed at him. Well, this was *his* territory—at least it was his father's.

"All this belongs to the Waterworks Authority. And no one's allowed here," he blurted out.

"But *you're* here!" Machiel remarked. He wasn't angry at all any more, but Allard was.

"You Veere people are against everything—against the dam and against the caissons. So what are you doing here? I know all about the trouble you people have started—I've heard all about it from my father."

"You're just like Wolfert," Machiel said. "He's always talking about his father too."

He smiled, and suddenly Allard smiled back. He really had a rather pleasant face, Machiel thought, but you could see he was used to defending himself.

"Well," Allard said. "It's true, isn't it, you're against everything. That's why I asked what you were doing here." He stuck his chin in the air and looked obstinately at the other boy. Machiel slung his leg over the bicycle seat.

"Is it any wonder," he said slowly. "Did they ever ask *us* about the dam? But those people . . . well I mean, they plunk themselves right down, and they go right ahead." He had been about to say "Those people from the Waterworks Authority," and Allard noticed that he *didn't* say it.

"Don't forget," Machiel continued, "they won't be able to fish here any more. And the water won't ebb and flow any more. And no one will be able to catch crayfish or shrimp. You've got to realize they're all going to have to move," he finished bitterly.

Allard shrugged. "Then they'll move. We move so often!"

"Yes, but that's different."

"Why?" For a moment the two boys looked at each other threateningly.

"Because." Both were silent.

"My mother drowned over there in the flood," Machiel said suddenly. Allard stepped back. Machiel nodded brusquely toward the sea, whose monotonous noise took on a threatening tone, and then pointed toward Kamperland, almost hidden beneath a gray mist.

Allard followed his glance. "I didn't know that," he mumbled uncomfortably.

"No. But that's why *I'm* not all that much against it," Machiel said. "At least with a dam things like that won't happen again. And you'll be able to fish in spite of it, Dingenis says."

Allard was silent, he didn't know what to say; he still had his mother.

"Where's your cap?" he asked, though he had really meant to say something quite different.

"Lost it someplace around here," Machiel answered vaguely. The mention of his cap made him think of his father again.

"It's bad for the others, of course," he said. "At home the whole thing causes more trouble every day. And Andries . . ." He was silent. Actually he had meant to say what an awful mood Andries's father was in these days, but he held back. He wouldn't like someone else to talk about what went on in *his* home. "What happens at home is nobody's business," his father always said, and Moei Katrina would always add: "You don't wash your dirty linen in public."

"What do you mean?" Allard asked curiously.

"Nothing. Well I mean things aren't what they ought to be at home either. Everyone's in a bad mood. They have to move, and there aren't even any houses for them to move to. My father's away all the time. He's on the Fishermen's Council, and they're always busy meeting someplace. They're always writing letters to The Hague. And now they've gone there themselves!"

Allard had a mocking reply all ready, something about that little handful of fishermen who expected the Prime Minister to do something for them. But Machiel was so upset that Allard said instead: "Things aren't what they ought to be at our house, either, you know. Do you think *I* ever get to see my father?"

Machiel looked up in surprise. "But he lives with you, doesn't he?"

"Sure," Allard replied. "But he's never home. First he spends weeks and weeks working alone before Mother and my sister Celestine and I can join him. And when he is home, people are always coming to talk to him—overseers and contractors and people like that. And they talk about the speed of the current in the Gap, and about flood tides and ebb tides and mattresses for the caissons. Sometimes I get sick and tired of it . . ."

As though he recognized something of himself in what Allard was saying, Machiel looked carefully at the other boy.

"When you're home," Allard said confidentially, "they haven't time for you. Whether they're busy with shrimp or the Delta Dams, it's six of one and a half dozen of the other. And what can you do about it? My father's crazy about his work."

"Yes. Mine too," Machiel agreed. "You know, I'll be glad when the dam is finished. At least the fuss will be over then."

"Won't do me much good, though," Allard remarked resignedly. "He'll just look around for another gap to put a dam into. Or a lock. Or a breakwater. Or a pier. That's the way it's always been."

Silently they looked into the distance. The rising water slammed against the dikes; you could see the flying whitecaps. Machiel thought of his father. Soon he and the rest of the family would be moving. None of them wanted it that way, and yet it seemed to be the only solution. He looked broodingly at the caissons rising steeply out of the gray earth.

"Magnificent, aren't they?" Allard said proudly, following Machiel's glance.

"Yes . . . Say! How do they sink them?" Machiel's tone was suddenly less distant.

"They use electromotors."

"Oh. And how do they get the things out there?"

Curiously Allard looked at him. Why would a fishing boy

be interested in such things? But his tone was casual as he explained:

"Well, you saw that all the caissons are being built in a ditch. They fill the ditch with water, and then they scoop out a trench alongside the small dike, all the way from the dry-dock to the dam. And then the caissons float out to the gap. The *Europa* and the *Asia,* the biggest tugboats in the world, will be here to haul them out."

Allard paused. Then he asked suddenly, "What are you going to be?"

"Fisherman," Machiel answered automatically, scratching his ear as if he were trying to remember something. "My cap! I almost forgot!" he said. They searched the ground together, but the cap wasn't there.

"Ask the gamekeeper's dog," Allard suggested, and Machiel looked up quickly. Both boys smiled. Things like that could be said now. A whistle sounded in the distance.

"There are the others. I've got to go," Machiel said. "But . . ."

"Well?" Both noticed how strained it sounded.

"I . . . uh . . . Maybe you'd like to see our boat?" Dingenis would have something unpleasant to say about that, but the *Ve 20* wasn't his alone.

"Yes, I would," Allard said. His voice was clear, and his eyes were happy. He was no longer the stiff, sulking boy who had stood in the road with an arrogant look. Suddenly Machiel felt an overwhelming desire to tell Allard all about their Plan. But he didn't. After all, The Plan was not his alone. Maybe later on, he thought.

"Then you'll come over sometime," Machiel said lightly. "But you'd better hurry," he added over his shoulder, "or your father will have the whole thing shut up so tight you won't be able to!" Deftly he dodged Allard's long arm which was about to hit him teasingly.

"Then you do something about it." Allard called.

Machiel raised his arm in farewell. He did not look for his cap again.

Allard laughed happily, watching his new friend go home.

9
THE GROWNUPS

"I SAW it with my own eyes!" Wolfert's face was redder than ever because Andries didn't believe him. The two stood facing Machiel in the Market Square, and the others waited curiously to see what would happen.

"Don't let them get your goat, Machiel! Wolfert's always making trouble," Tannie said, but she couldn't budge Andries; he stared at Machiel, wondering what to believe. Machiel hadn't stayed away all that time looking for his cap; he had met the boy from the Waterworks Authority. Not only had he met him, but the two had stood talking while the group had been waiting.

"And here we thought you were looking for your cap!" Andries said crossly. "We waited for you!"

The others were staring too, Machiel saw, waiting for him to say something. But he refused to explain what had happened. He pulled his red and white polka dot handkerchief out of his pocket and put it back again, folding it carefully. He shrugged his shoulders and looked at the Town Hall gables.

"My cap wasn't there," he said. "And the boy was just riding by. That's all."

"What did he say?" Adriana asked inquisitively.

"I'll bet he told you the caissons were his!" Andries cried. "And we had no business being there. Those people are all the same. Tough as nails, my father says. And they always act as if·the whole show belongs to them."

"You're just as bad as Wolfert," Machiel said bitterly.

"That's got nothing to do with it!" Andries cried, and Wolfert nodded emphatically. It couldn't do him any harm if Andries and Machiel quarreled.

"Did you actually see them yourself?" Tannie asked sharply.

"What do you think!" Wolfert snapped back. "I was last because I was having trouble with my bicycle seat. You know that."

How convenient, Tannie thought.

"Well, I looked around to see if Machiel had found his cap, and I saw the stuck-up kid himself."

"He's a perfectly ordinary boy," Machiel observed. "And may I ask if I need your permission to talk to someone?" He didn't raise his voice at all, but there was something in it that left the others stunned and silent. Only Wolfert dared to continue:

"A perfectly ordinary kid? I'll say! But he and his father are the ones who'll chase you out of here pretty soon."

"That's none of your business!" Tannie shot at him. Machiel looked at Wolfert slowly; he knew exactly what the farm boy was up to, and it wouldn't be the first time he had tried to cause trouble between friends. He glanced at Andries, who was silent.

"And then pretending you're still with us and The Plan,"

Wolfert baited him. "Of course you blabbed it all to that boy," he finished maliciously.

Machiel took his hands out of his pockets slowly, but he still didn't say anything. Neither did Andries, who stood looking at Machiel closely, a frown on his freckled face. Tannie saw that her brother had driven a wedge between Machiel and Andries. Machiel was too obstinate to talk about the stranger, and Andries was jealous. She was furious with her brother; she would have loved to hit him over the head.

"There's Arjaan," Adriana cried. She pretended to be delighted and stepped away from the little circle to wave to him. But the man was already coming toward them. Paying no attention to Tannie's sigh of relief or Wolfert's furious face he walked right into the center of the group.

"We got a call from The Hague. Your father," he nodded at Machiel. And suddenly the boy relaxed. Holding his head high, he looked at the others. His father had gone to The Hague today, for Veere.

"Machieeeeel! Machieeeeel!" Sjakie called shrilly. The child dashed around the corner on his clattering wooden shoes, straight to his brother's arms. "Nobody's home! Moei Katrina's gone too!" Machiel held the boy close while he listened.

"They had coffee with the Prime Minister," Arjaan told them. "And he said he'd think it over. Maybe they'll come and have a look themselves. Mr. Maris was there."

"Never heard of him," Wolfert muttered.

"Well, he's one of them," Arjaan said, not quite sure, really, just who he was. "Why don't you read the papers!" he challenged.

The children snorted. The newspapers!

"But what are they going to think over, Arjaan?" Andries asked eagerly.

"The sluice gate."

"But the dam is going to be built then?"

"Well, yes." The old man's voice sounded tired. "There wasn't much to be done about that. But the men of Veere certainly were able to make the consequences clear."

"The water won't ebb and flow any more . . . There won't be any jellyfish . . ." Wolfert lamented.

"A lot of difference that'll make to you! You can't even swim!" Tannie shouted, and someone snickered.

No one noticed that Arjaan had left. Andries was stony silent, and only Tannie saw the anger in his eyes.

"Well *I'm* against it," she said.

"Against what?"

"Against . . . against everything! Against the Delta Plan. And against the sailboats. I like fishing boats much better. They *belong* here! And then . . ."

"And then what?" Andries asked her sharply. Shyly, Tannie looked at the ground.

"In summer they'll have to go all the way to Colijn to be with their fathers. And that's more than two and a half hours from here by boat!"

Nobody asked who "they" were, but Machiel and Andries gave each other a friendly glance.

"Yes," said Machiel. "But after all it's worse for our fathers. They'll only be able to come home once a week."

"That Mr. Maris ought to live here and have a shrimp boat and be chased out to stupid old Colijn," Tannie said angrily. "I'd love to see his face then."

"Prime Ministers don't have shrimp boats," Machiel said. "You ought to know that."

"But what does he do all day?" she asked. A loud sigh from Machiel told her he had heard enough. "What difference does it make, anyway?" he said savagely. He meant to the others, who did not come from fishermen's families, and to whom this was all a game, like The Plan. But Andries, thoroughly upset by everything, misunderstood. He whirled about so quickly that both he and Machiel stumbled against the little blue stoop of Mrs. Hubregse's store, tripping over the milk box she had put out for the milkman.

The tall green door flew open with a violent slam, and the children shrank from the shrill voice bursting out above their heads:

"Get out of here! That's all I need! First you come clumping about here with your filthy wooden shoes. And as if that wasn't enough, you upset my milk box. *I* heard you! Saying the dam won't make any difference! Shame on you! You! A fisherman's son saying things like that! Do you have any idea what the dam out there is going to mean to me? Do you? The fishermen buy their supplies here—you ought to know that!"

She looked at the overturned milk box, its stream of white liquid pouring over the threshold, and all of a sudden she burst into tears. In dead silence, she wiped her wrinkled face on her apron.

Clumsily Machiel picked up the box. They were all used to scolding, even blows—but crying . . .

"We should . . . We wanted to . . ." He didn't know what to say. Not two hours before they had been so impressed by the enormous caissons they had completely forgotten their purpose. The caissons were so huge that even The Plan seemed silly and unimportant. But Mrs. Hubregse's tears made them feel they had betrayed the fishermen. Machiel and Andries shuffled their shoes on the uneven stones.

At that very moment Wolfert came dashing around the corner. None of them had seen him leave the group.

"Hey! You've got to hear what Jacob says!" he yelled in excitement.

"Where were you?" Andries cried. In a flash he had forgotten the store and the milk box and Mrs. Hubregse, who stopped crying to listen to the news. She dropped a corner of her apron just enough to show her brown eyes with all their wrinkles. But when Wolfert reported, "The movie makers are coming next month!" she exploded again.

"Get off my stoop! You don't know anything! You don't have any sense!" she yelled.

"She's upset about the boats," Andries explained. He felt uncomfortable, because he could understand that Mrs. Hubregse would find the changes very hard to take.

Slowly all the children except Machiel started to leave. A decent distance from the store they suddenly broke into a run, screaming and dashing through the town. Machiel stayed, looking down at the ground, displeased with himself and with the rest of the world.

"Get lost!" he bellowed at Sjakie, who hung onto him. The little boy started with fright. Machiel cursed himself for being so cruel, but he didn't know how to apologize. Abruptly he turned on his heel, angry because he was angry without good cause, and angrier that he had taken it out on his brother. He was upset by all the confusion—thoughts of Allard, the great caissons, Mrs. Hubregse and his father.

"A person who's confused himself must first set his own house in order," his father always said, "or others will suffer the consequences." Right, Machiel thought, but if Father only knew all the things he had on his mind!

One day can be so different from the next. Some days drag by, and everything goes wrong. Other days the sun shines for you alone; then you can't understand how you could ever have been upset.

Machiel sat on his haunches on the deck of the *Ve 20*. Tourists swarmed over the quay, but he didn't turn to watch. Now and then, the thick mending needle in his hand, he looked through the nets and the thin, upright masts toward the sea, glittering behind him in the soft February sun.

Sjakie sat next to him, and when Machiel glanced at him, he hummed a little tune. Jacob, Andries's older brother, had given Machiel a bottle of apple juice; half of it was for Andries, and Sjakie would get part of the other half. Tenderly, he looked at his brother's little face beneath his father's cap. Machiel felt his own head. He hadn't found his cap. Well, he wouldn't think about it now. Sjakie leaned forward, dangling his short arm overboard. Machiel saw his index finger following the flight of a huge bluebottle shimmering in the sun and buzzing the ship. Now and then the fly would hover in the air and nervously rub its forelegs before buzzing along.

"What were you before you were a little boy, Machiel?" Sjakie asked. And before his brother could answer he whispered, "I was a seal! But Moei Katrina won't believe me!"

Machiel looked at his brother and grinned. A boy like that was so small, he thought. Yet, in a couple of years, Sjakie would be big. And he and Dingenis would be grown men. How strange it all was.

"When I have my own ship, will you be my partner?" Machiel asked. Sjakie merely nodded, but Machiel was content. He picked up his needle again and set about mending the hole.

"Machiel!"

He looked up startled to see who had called. It was Allard, watching him from the quay. His greeting was a bit uncertain, as though he didn't quite know what sort of reception he would get. All at once Machiel saw his ship as Allard must be seeing it, the row of cutters behind them, men and boys all working busily.

"Hi, there!" Allard said.

"Hi," Machiel answered, smiling tentatively.

"What are you doing?"

"Mending nets."

"Oh."

Both of them looked down the quay. "Want to come on board?" Machiel asked. Allard lost no time, winking at Sjakie who stared icily at the stranger.

Picking up a shrimp, Allard asked, "Can you clean shrimp, too?"

"Of course," Machiel answered. Suddenly Wolfert's cutting voice sounded from the crowd along the quay:

"Just look at that! Great friends now, aren't they?"

Machiel was furious. Leave me alone, he wished urgently, but Wolfert didn't budge.

"They're babysitting together!" he yelled, louder still. A passer-by snickered, and slowly Machiel got to his feet. Wolfert snarled at him, but before anyone else could move, Allard had grabbed a bucket of water from the deck and thrown half of it at Wolfert's legs. The boy gave a scream and jumped back, right onto the toes of an elegant gentleman, who snatched up his tripod furiously and grabbed Wolfert by the neck. Sjakie shrieked with laughter, his cap tumbling down over his ears. Machiel grinned too, but when he saw Allard's look of triumph as he dried his hands, he said stiffly:

"You didn't need to do that. I can fight my own battles."

"Sure," said Allard. "But your hands were tied up in nets."

Allard seemed a bit more at ease and remarked, "They're not much, those guys."

"Oh, well . . ." Machiel couldn't actually say there were others besides Wolfert—like Tannie and Andries Domisse. Andries! Goodness! He had almost forgotten they had agreed to go fishing on the jetty. He peered through the curtains of nets to the *Tho 16* where Andries was helping out. Andries's face was turned in Machiel's direction, and at the same time Andries was looking up at the deck hand who stood talking to him. Allard watched Machiel carefully, then he turned again toward the tall houses with their blue-gray shutters and their steep gables, and to the mighty, massive towers.

"Some church you have here," he remarked. "Why is it so huge?"

"Just because," Machiel said, thinking of Andries.

"Don't you ever get bored around here?"

"Bored?" Machiel's only answer was to look at the translucent sea-green water. "The Queen is the marchioness of Veere," he said out of the blue.

"That doesn't help her much," Allard replied. He looked at Machiel, busy frowning over his nets. That time on the road things had seemed so much easier, so much more natural.

Then Allard asked, "How do you do that?" He pointed at the pile of nets and the needle in Machiel's hand.

"Just like this. You hold the net together, and then you pull —like this." The two boys bent together over the net.

Sjakie had fallen fast asleep, and on the quay footsteps hurried to and fro.

"Hello there!" a man called. The boys looked up surprised.

"It's my father," Machiel said, looking proudly at Allard, who carefully took in the big, strong man in the navy blue skipper's uniform and the youth with the woolen cap walking next to him.

"Your brother?" Allard asked.

"Dingenis," Machiel answered. Dingenis had nodded too—a bit curtly, Machiel thought. Suddenly Machiel saw Andries coming toward him, stepping over the decks of the two cutters between the *Ve 20* and the *Tho 16*. Machiel glanced uncomfortably at Allard. How was he going to show him the ship when he had promised to go fishing with Andries? But just then Allard looked at his watch and announced: "Hey! I've got to go. So long!" He leaped off the boat onto the quay and walked off, whistling loudly as Andries stepped onto the deck over Sjakie's sleeping head.

"So," was all Andries said. But he looked at Machiel as he had that afternoon in the square.

"Jacob gave me some apple juice," Machiel told him.

"I've had some," Andries said.

Machiel opened the bottle and drank, gurgling loudly. He forgot he was supposed to leave some for Sjakie, emptied the whole bottle in one gulp and set it down triumphantly.

"Playing up to that boy, huh?" Andries said with great restraint.

"Don't be silly," Machiel replied.

"Well I couldn't care less. Do as you please." The whole deck wobbled with the mighty leap that Andries took onto the quay. Casually he yelled back, "Oh, by the way, I can't go fishing this evening. So long!"

Machiel stared after his friend, who walked toward the Tower with long, angry steps.

10
AT THE
CONSTRUCTION SITE

It was almost spring, and the trees on the quay were soft and green. The busloads of tourists had started coming again, full of people wearing cameras and sunglasses. All the tourists gathered on the quay when the fishing boats returned. And they did return faithfully every afternoon, except for a week now and then, maybe two weeks, when they fished in Scheveningen and couldn't come home quite so often. They sailed out and they sailed in. Everything was the same.

The grownups had gone to The Hague, and a couple of weeks later had heard the results of their discussion with the Prime Minister. "A dam without a sluice gate for Veere is a hard fate"—that was their slogan, but it had not helped. There would be no sluice gate.

The government had said it would be too dangerous. If the dam had a sluice gate, the terrific current pouring through at that one point might smash one of the caissons. No, the dam would be completely closed. Their last hope gone, the fishermen slowly started planning their move to Colijnsplaat. Their reactions varied. Machiel's father was calm, quieter than ever. Skipper Domisse was bitter, cursing now and then when things were too much for him. Old Arjaan was sad and muttered to himself a lot, walking down the quay. Youths like Dingenis and Jacob were matter-of-fact, even devil-may-care.

The sixth grade had not returned to the caissons. And the members of the group were not as close as they once had been. Perhaps it was because of the coolness between Machiel and Andries. Or maybe it was because the stranger was still in the class. All of them were used to Allard van Beusekom by now, but they still called him "the stranger," and he was still an outsider. They didn't have anything to do with him, and he was only a little less lonely than he had been his first day. Only Machiel ever sought him out. He had been to Allard's house a couple of times, and Allard had been amazed at the fishing boy's curiosity about anything connected with hydraulic engineering, his fascination with sketches and sea current charts which Allard's father sometimes left lying around his study. The boys got along well together, and Machiel clearly took Allard's part when Wolfert or any of the others annoyed him. But Allard still had the feeling that Machiel was holding back, as if he were afraid of what his friends would say.

Never, even during vacation time, had Veere been as busy as now. More and more newsmen, photographers and ordinary people swarmed into town. The dam seemed to have come to life, and across the glittering water the seven caissons were ready and inexpressibly threatening. Tourists sitting and eating behind the thick tower pointed westward; never before had they seen anything more impressive.

One fine morning at the height of all this hubbub, a newsman pulled into town in a flashy red sports car. Not only did he want to see the caissons, but he also wanted to know everything about the fishermen and their families.

"Good morning, sir," Machiel heard his father say, and the boy peeked out, noticing that Gilles, too, was taking the man in sharply. Gilles glanced at Machiel with immediate understanding: "From the papers," he said.

Machiel began fiddling with a net so it wouldn't look as if he were eavesdropping. His father and the reporter were talking about Colijnsplaat.

"All right—we'll move," Machiel heard his father say. "It makes sense, doesn't it? But is it all that simple?"

"It's not just the cost. But those of us who are Catholics have no church there. They'll have to go all the way to Goes. And take my brother-in-law's two children. They'll have to go to school in Goes. And what about the girls in teacher's college? Where are they supposed to go? Will he have to take them out of school? Or board them here in Veere? He's going to have to go to Colijnsplaat himself. And then there's no harbor. The bollards are no good. You can't get right up close with your ship."

"What are bollards?" the reporter asked.

"Posts. You moor up against them," Machiel's father answered briefly.

"Oh. You went to The Hague, didn't you?"

"Yes. And I must say those gentlemen listened carefully to us, even though I had to explain about the bollards to Mr. Maris. Well anyway, they were prepared to come down by special car and see for themselves. But anything more than that . . ." Skipper Cevaal stared into the distance over his son's head.

The newsman put his notebook away.

"It hurts you to have to leave Veere," he said softly.

Skipper Cevaal looked at the reporter. "I was born here," he said stiffly. "So was my father. We've always sailed from here. That's not a small matter. And my sons, they'll want the same thing. One of them has already gone to fishing school, and the other is going in September." Machiel heard the pride in his father's voice, and his heart sank like a stone. Why? Wasn't it true? "My sons want the same thing."

Suddenly the newsman burst out: "Can't something be done? You still have six weeks . . ."

". . . seven . . ."

". . . seven weeks to get a new engine put in?"

"Yes, or I'll never make it from Colijn to the fishing grounds," Skipper Cevaal explained.

"But who's paying for it?"

"Well, I am. I have to."

"Will you get the money back?"

"Maybe some of it. They were talking about interest-free loans."

"Haven't there been any protest demonstrations?" the reporter asked. Machiel looked at his father. Was he going to explode now? About all the meetings? And letters? And protests? But his father only said:

"Oh, yes. Many of them. Protests, demonstrations. The Fishermen's Council has worked hard. But for what? They're going ahead anyway." He spoke without bitterness.

"So many people have come here, and they want to know everything—when we're moving, what sort of compensation we're getting. But we don't know any more than you can read in the newspapers. When we sail out for the last time the Burgomaster wants to sound the bells. And a Mr. Haanstra is supposed to film it all. But really, a fisherman doesn't care much for all that."

Machiel banged his head as he shot up at the word "film." It had never been clearer to him that something must be done. He blurted out, "We won't be made fools of!"

"Better leave that to me," his father said, more sharply than Machiel expected. "And take this gentleman over to see Aunt Sanne."

Machiel eyed the red sports car. Imagine riding in that! He hoped Andries would see him.

"Climb in!" the reporter said, smiling. Together they drove past the Town Hall.

"What are you going to be?" the newsman suddenly asked. Machiel looked away quickly and hesitated. Did grownups know what you were thinking? That you were turning things over in your mind slowly, so slowly that sometimes you didn't know yourself what you really wanted?

"Fisherman," he answered shortly. "This is where Aunt Sanne lives." She'll certainly have plenty to say, Machiel thought. Of all the women around Veere, his aunt was the most prickly.

When they went inside, Mrs. Bouterse looked at the reporter suspiciously. He gave his name—Klaassen.

"Newspaper? Oh, about the dam. Well, mister, *I've* never been near there! I say we could have best done without it. The disaster of '53? Yes, but listen now—you're talking about things that hardly ever happen. You don't have to think of the worst possible things all the time. *I* don't find the dam strictly necessary. They needn't have wrung the fishing industry's neck. In ten years the very same thing will happen over there, when they close the East Schelde."

"Then you're going to Colijn too?" Mr. Klaassen asked, when Machiel's aunt stopped for breath.

"Never! Not as long as I live! We just bought a house here—practically on the quay. You think they're waiting for us with open arms in Colijn? They haven't built a single house there yet! And what sort of compensation will we get?" she demanded threateningly. "We don't even know anything about that for sure. It's a disgrace!"

"Do you get along well with your aunt?" Klaassen asked as he and Machiel returned to the car.

"Oh, no! Never! And she's always complaining about the disaster," Machiel told him.

"It's pretty hard to take, you know," the man said, excusing her. "In 1953 they were driven out of Schouwen-en-Duiveland by the flood. Now they're being driven out of Veere by a dam. A person can get bitter because of all that, except that being bitter never helped anyone." Machiel looked at the reporter in amazement. How did this man who had barely met his aunt know so much about her?

"People are gradually getting to know about the Delta Plan," Mr. Klaassen went on, "but they have to know how it is for ordinary people too. What do you think of it?" He looked at Machiel so insistently that he blushed. Ever since Machiel had heard about the work of hydraulic engineers like Allard's father, he had found fishing far less fascinating than before. But how could he tell a stranger that? He'd have to watch his step.

"It's tough on the fishermen, you know," he said, dodging the issue. "But it's safer for the others." In the mirror he saw the man grinning at him, and it made him strangely angry.

"Will you come with me to get a look at the caissons?" Klaassen asked unexpectedly. Machiel was shocked. Should I go or not? he wondered.

"I could," he said slowly.

They raced across the quay, past the orange and blue lifeboat and past the muddy last bit of harbor. Then they turned into the road to the Vrouwen polder, and when they caught sight of the caissons, Mr. Klaassen stopped with a jerk.

"It's absolutely unbelievable!" the man exclaimed. "How will they ever get those things out of here?"

"Easy," Machiel answered. "When it's time they'll tear the little retaining dike down. The construction ditch will fill with water, and the caissons will float. Then the *Europa* and the *Asia* will come along and haul them off."

The reporter looked at the fishing boy with undisguised amazement. "How do you know all that?" he asked. "You're supposed to know all about ships and shrimp, aren't you?"

"I have a friend with the Waterworks Authority," Machiel said carelessly. He moved away a little when he saw Klaassen's face. Roaring with laughter the man turned the car and stepped down on the gas. "He's got a friend with the Waterworks Authority!" he chortled. "Well, it so happens I have an appointment at the construction site. Can you show me the way?"

Machiel forgot his annoyance, and his face brightened. "Okay," he said.

The road climbed up over the dunes, and on the other side a policeman stood with his arm raised in the air.

"Where are you going, sir?"

"We have an appointment with the Waterworks Authority," Klaassen said through the window. The policeman saluted and waved them through.

The reporter looked about intently at the asphalt and stone, the tremendous caissons in the distance, the scoops and concrete mixers near the water, the swaying cranes and shouting workmen, the beams and blocks of basalt, the long pipes laid out on the grass.

Klaassen parked at the brown wooden shack with the sign *Government Waterworks Authority,* and disappeared inside. Machiel eyed the building from all sides. So this was headquarters, he thought.

To the right was the Gap. Never had he seen it so close up, not even those nights he had sailed past it. He walked up the wooden path to the shack, stumbling over a piece of basalt. Should he go in? If anyone stopped him he could say he was looking for Mr. Klaassen. Carefully Machiel pushed open the door of the little building. There was a long brown corridor, smelling of wood stain. And there was no one in sight. The corridor widened into a sort of hallway. And right in the middle was an absolutely enormous model of the Veere Gap and the new dam. A low whistle broke from Machiel as he caught sight of it. He forgot his fears and came right up to the huge wooden table. Here, in all its detail, was the answer to the question he had asked himself for weeks: How did they do it? He knew all about the Veere Gap and its sand bars. He knew the Gap at least as well as his father did. And all the treacherous currents. You could see them clearly painted here one alongside the other—blue, dark blue and green. Here—that must be Restless Flats. And this was the area known as the Herring Chomper. At ebb tide the sand bar would be above water. What was that? Oh, the floor of the sea at the closing point of the dam. Allard called the area a threshold, like the threshold in a doorway, and Machiel thought that a logical name. There had to be something they could set the heavy caissons on if they didn't want them just to sink into the mud. First a woven nylon mattress was put down and stretched out on the threshold to protect it against the churning of the water. Carefully, Machiel bent forward and touched the model with his fingers. The threshold sloped up a bit toward the middle. It was so real! He hadn't yet taken in the whole model, and it wasn't until this moment that he caught sight of the seven miniature caissons next to one another in a row. Every detail had been reproduced; even the wooden portcullises were there. Those doors that opened and closed vertically always intrigued Machiel. He tried them out. So that was how they pulled them up, and then they were let down again—like that. Easy! You could almost do it yourself. Oh, lord! One of them was sticking. Machiel jerked at it nervously. He didn't notice that the door behind him had opened.

"Pssst! Machieeeeel!" The voice gave him such a fright he looked about in blank amazement.

"Machiel—you nut!" the same voice hissed at him, and suddenly a boy appeared out of the darkness of the corridor.

"Allard!" cried Machiel, as his fright caught up with him. "What—what are you doing here?" He swallowed hard a couple of times.

"Oh, come on! I should ask *you* that!"

"I . . ." Machiel wiped his forehead with the back of his hand. Now Allard would see he'd been fooling with the caisson door, and his father . . .

"The overseer down there asked me to bring my father a message," Allard explained.

"Tell me what to do with this," Machiel begged, all flustered and upset. "The little door . . . I just touched it by accident and . . ."

"Little door! It's a portcullis," Allard corrected him.

"I know!" Machiel exclaimed. The longer it took the more nervous he got, and at that very moment a door opened, and the voices of two men could be heard coming closer and closer.

"See! It's too late now!" Machiel hissed. Now he'd really get in trouble.

"Pssst! Wait—I'll . . . It's my father." Allard whispered, moving closer to Machiel. "Keep looking at that thing," Allard commanded. The boys studied the wooden waves of the Veere Gap. Behind them the voices drew nearer.

"No danger . . . not yet. And there won't be any once the caissons are in place. The only danger will occur while the closing point is being filled with caissons, one by one. That's obvious." Mr. van Beusekom spoke matter-of-factly. Then Klaassen asked, "Why?"

"Because the currents change direction as the caissons are set in. Each caisson that is added makes the Gap narrower, you see, and that speeds up the currents enormously. The force of the water becomes extremely dangerous, and eddies could develop on the threshold. The first caisson will be a sort of trial run. A week later all six remaining ones will go in, one after the other, one each day."

Now the voices and the steps were just around the corner. The boys kept staring at the wooden waves.

"That seventh one will be exciting," the reporter remarked. Now both men stood still.

"Yes. It's the first great Delta closing, an operation that all of Holland will be watching every minute." Pride sounded in the engineer's cool voice. Mr. Klaassen cleared his throat. "Of course for Veere it's a terrible thing." Machiel pricked up his ears at this, but he didn't dare move.

The footsteps sounded again.

"It's really for the best," Mr. van Beusekom replied. "They think there's nothing outside of Veere, nothing of any importance beside their Town Hall and their Towers and their fishermen. It *won't* be the end of the fishermen, I can tell you. All that moaning about poor Veere. Do you know what almost happened here in the flood of 1953? And what *did* happen over there?" A jacket sleeve grazed briefly against a window, and Machiel knew that Allard's father was pointing toward Kamperland. He probably didn't know that Machiel's mother had died there, but it almost sounded as if he *did* know and wanted to build a dam here for that reason alone, so that mothers would be safe in the future. Mothers and children. Imagine working at something as magnificent as that! Machiel thought.

Mr. van Beusekom's voice sounded quite close, and Machiel stared at the model, hardly daring to move.

"Let me show you all this on the model . . ."

Machiel froze, but his eyes turned carefully to Allard standing right behind him, hiding the broken portcullis.

"What? Haven't you gone home yet?" Mr. van Beusekom asked. "And who's this? Don't you know, Allard, that no one under the age of fourteen is allowed in here?"

"It's Machiel!" Allard said quickly. "From Veere." The engineer turned to Machiel and asked:

"Are you Allard's friend?"

"Uh . . . we . . . yes, sir . . . Mr. . . ." Machiel stuttered. How did one address an engineer? Klaassen appeared behind Allard's father. "He *does* have a friend with the Waterworks! I thought it was a dodge so he'd be able to come snooping around here."

"He did come," Mr. van Beusekom pointed out coolly, and his eyes lit on the broken portcullis. "Why did you have to fool with that, child?" he asked, rather harshly. Allard was about to say something, but his father stopped him with a sign. Machiel felt sick and helpless.

"I . . . I . . . I wanted to . . ." He broke out in a sweat. "I wanted to see!" he blurted out suddenly.

"What did you want to see?" The man's tone was mocking. "You people from Veere never want to have anything to do with the dam, do you? They've told me in a thousand ways a thousand times since I've been here that we're not doing them any good, that we won't be welcome at the celebration when the last ships sail out and that they just want to be left alone to fish. What do you do?"

"Go to school."

"He's a fisherman," Allard broke in.

"Is that so?" The engineer's voice was dry. And then Machiel remembered what his father always told him: "Look people straight in the eye—even if you're afraid of them. You'll see—your fears will disappear."

It was true. As he raised his head and met the piercing black eyes of Mr. van Beusekom, he heard himself say quietly:

"Veere people never come here, and most of the boys couldn't care less. But I wanted to find out how it's done."

Suddenly there was something in the face opposite him that made Machiel think of his own father.

"You mean how a dam is built?"

"Yes. How the portcullises work. And how it's possible—seven of them in that gap—the last one I mean. Well, one of them is broken. I'll . . ."

There was silence in the little room. Slowly Mr. van Beusekom looked from one boy's face to the other. His son stood waiting trustingly; Machiel was still a little tense, and a frown wrinkled his forehead.

The engineer's voice was suddenly normal. "It's very simple," he explained. "The separation dike between the dry dock and the water outside is broken through. We drive the seven caissons up one by one and place them on the ground in the gap. The wooden guards over the steel portcullises are removed on the sea side. Look, like this!" Pointing at the broken portcullis he laughed. "One of them has already been removed. And then we hoist the steel portcullis to let the tide through as usual. Then we have to calculate just when to let the portcullises down again. They all go down simultaneously, and then the sea is permanently closed off."

"But how does it work?" Machiel insisted.

"What?"

"I mean the water. The water is so terribly strong. And you put the caissons right across the current, with a big piece of them right in the sea. That time when the flood came the water was so strong . . ."

Mr. van Beusekom looked at the boy. Then he said:

"That's probably the trickiest part of the whole operation. Come along. I'll explain it to you."

They walked through the building until they reached the door which said *Van Beusekom, Chief Engineer*. Inside, maps, charts full of squiggly lines, tide tables, drawings of scoops, concrete mixers and pumps hung on every square inch of the walls. The tables and chests were covered with pages of calculations, illustrations and sketches of the threshold and the caissons, with and without the portcullises: portcullis open, portcullis closed . . .

So this was where it all went on, Machiel thought. But "they" sat on plain ordinary chairs. "They" smoked cigarettes and talked, and they weren't such monsters as one would have thought. They were really quite ordinary people, but they were people who were strenuously at work on something important. Machiel felt the decision he had been thinking about begin to catch fire in him again. Perhaps that was what he really wanted—to work with others on defenses against the devastating water. He bent over the paper on which Allard's father was sketching the dike, the water and the closing point of the gap. He listened to Mr. van Beusekom explaining briefly and clearly:

"You see, it has to be early in the year. The contractors have to have as much time as possible to finish the dam before the winter storms. Tons of stone are necessary, and millions of yards of sand must be moved before a dike becomes a dike. Here is the tide forecast. You have to figure on spring tides and neap tides too. But you know as much as I do about that. And now I'll show you how the caissons turn on hinges . . ."

Patiently Allard's father explained all aspects of the construction of the dam. He talked about how men become engineers, too. "Don't think they make it in a week," he said. "They begin by just measuring things—current strengths and silting rates. They measure dunes and calculate the rate of erosion. Sometimes they live in a house and sometimes in a wooden shack. Well, that's enough for now. I've talked too long already! But here, take this book. You might like to read it. It will tell you a lot more about dikes and the water."

"Thank you! Thank you very much!" Machiel exclaimed, letting his excitement show. Then he said goodby to Allard, and he and Mr. Klaassen headed back to Veere.

11
THE FILM MAKER

KLAASSEN dropped Machiel off at the Market Square. As he stepped out of the sports car and nodded politely to the reporter, Andries came racing up, more elated than he had been in weeks. He waved his arms wildly and burst out with his news even before he reached Machiel.

"The man's here for the movie!"

"Where?" Machiel asked. But Andries was so out of breath that he merely waved one arm furiously at the quay and with the other beckoned the rest of the gang running toward them down Market Street. A few hundred feet ahead of them was a little group of men, the Burgomaster in the middle.

"They've been walking through Veere for a whole hour," Andries reported, still panting. "And they were received at the Town Hall. The whole Town Council was there."

"I don't know anything about it," Wolfert remarked sharply. Then he caught sight of the book Machiel was carrying and said, "Oh, reading about dams, eh? Where did you get that?"

Machiel could see what was going to happen. They would start arguing about the dam again, and he and Andries would be driven even further apart. His head was whirling from everything Allard's father had explained to him. Glancing at Andries, he thought, maybe I will decide to become an engineer, but that's my business. And anyway, they still don't have the right to make the movie. As calmly as he could he said, "Look, are we going to talk about this book, or are we going to find a way to talk to the movie man? He's not going to be here forever, you know. How did you find out he was here?"

None of the children had ever heard Machiel speak so sharply. Andries was hurt, but for the moment he, too, was more interested in the movie. "Arjaan saw them coming. And then I came up—down. I mean I wanted to keep an eye on them. And then I saw you too. And so." Andries's speech was jumbled, but Machiel looked at him happily. He was hot-tempered, but he was a good friend.

"Come along behind them," Andries whispered. "But keep back, hear? They mustn't catch sight of us."

Showing nothing in their faces, the children marched along, a respectful distance behind the gentlemen.

The Burgomaster's voice was vibrant. "Commercial fishermen sailed from this harbor. We have sent whale fishermen all the way to Greenland . . ."

"We? I didn't have anything to do with it," Joris mumbled.

"Keep still," Andries hissed. Tannie bit her lip, holding back a nervous giggle.

"We've got to talk to him," Andries whispered urgently.

"We *will* talk to him," Machiel said soothingly.

"But they've been walking around for more than an hour,"

Andries replied. "And all they're doing is staring at houses. I'm starving to death. I've been watching them all morning."

Almost as if they had heard, the little group disappeared into the Campveerse Tower with the Burgomaster.

"They're going to have lunch," Wolfert observed.

"Listen, if he's with the Burgomaster it won't work," Machiel said. "Wouldn't be polite. So why don't we do what they're doing? Let's take off, and we'll see them this afternoon. Veere isn't that big."

Andries hesitated, but finally the rumbling of his stomach broke down his resistance.

"There's something to what Machiel says," he finally decided. "Okay. Let's go. First we eat! But don't spend more than fifteen minutes at it. Then we'll all meet here again. If we're in luck . . ."

They *were* in luck. That afternoon Machiel discovered the producer standing all alone on the quay. Carefully he beckoned to the others, who were keeping watch along the wharf. And when they had all gathered, Machiel coughed pointedly. Slowly, the stranger looked up at the children, but he did not put on a special expression to listen to them. He acted as though he were dealing with adults. It wasn't at all difficult for Machiel and Andries to explain their idea to him, briefly and clearly, for Mr. Haanstra knew how to listen without interrupting. Only at the end of their story did he say:

"Well, yes . . . I can understand you would want to go along. But I have a contract to film the last sailing just as usual. And 'usually' children don't go along, do they?"

"Yes, but this is going to be different, sir!" Tannie said eagerly.

"After all, it's the last time," Andries pleaded. "After that they won't ever go through there again!"

"And, uh, we could help you on board," Machiel added. But now the man laughed, his white teeth gleaming in his brown face.

"Well, I've got my crew for that. I really have to go," Mr. Haanstra said. "But I'll think about it. Children coming along . . . yes . . . yes . . . it'll be . . ." The children held their breaths while he thought aloud:

"There's something to it . . . The older and the younger generations . . . The fishermen and their sons . . . The changes that will affect the youngsters too . . ." He turned toward them: "And do your fathers approve of the idea?"

"Well . . . they . . . we'll manage that, of course." Andries babbled. They hadn't planned that far ahead yet. "But I'm sure they'll approve."

"After all, they're our fathers, aren't they?" Wolfert said.

"Yes . . . yes . . . there's something to it . . ." the producer said, looking over their heads.

"We ought to be on those ships, isn't that right, sir?" Wolfert pleaded innocently.

"Sure, sure," the man replied, suddenly gripped by a mental picture. "Yes, yes, there's something to it . . ." he said as he walked away.

"It's working!" Andries rubbed his hands and nudged Machiel, who grinned too. But Tannie looked thoughtfully toward the jetty:

"You know, it's a shame. He's got such a nice face . . ."

"Oh, come on!" Andries turned on her indignantly. "No nonsense. What he looks like has nothing to do with it. Let's go find out what they think of it."

The fishermen did not object to the idea. In fact, they agreed almost too quickly, the boys thought. Andries was disappointed because he had at least four or five arguments ready in his mind. But Skipper Bouterse, weary and resigned, simply said:

"Oh, all right. What's the difference!" The other fishermen on the deck of the *Ve 20* looked just as uninterested. It was five o'clock, and all the ships were in. You could sense the blue mood on everyone.

"Let them come along!" a cheerful voice suddenly bellowed from the forecastle. "A couple more or less!" It was Dingenis.

"What's the idea? Want to load up my whole boat?" Skipper Cevaal asked. "I won't have any strangers on my boat that day. Machiel and Sjakie, okay. And Andries. But no one else, and that's final." Moei Katrina walked up, but she didn't say anything.

Dingenis shrugged.

"What's the difference?" he said, repeating Bouterse's words. "There'll be a wild scene here anyway that day. Those students from Utrecht still want to come along. They say their fraternity was named after Veere." He shrugged again. "Look, what do you care!"

"They have nothing at all to do with Veere," Skipper Domisse exploded. "Just a lot of ruckus and tomfoolery—that's all they want—all of them! I agree completely with Cevaal. They're going to stay off my ship! And those filming gentlemen won't get anywhere near it either! And I'll see to it that that scheming pack of blackguards from The Hague stays off my ship. The need for fresh water—huh! Did *we* ever complain about the salt in the earth? The farmers are always making trouble, but *they* get to stay. For the fishermen it's a matter of life and death. You've been to The Hague twice already! And what good did it do? None!"

Skipper Cevaal didn't say a word, but his face was so set that even Skipper Domisse thought it wise to stop for a moment. He stared bitterly into the distance and mumbled something to himself. Then he turned back to Skipper Cevaal accusingly:

"You even sweetly promised 'full cooperation' for that film producer, and it'll be just a pleasant little diversion for him. Yes, I heard all about it. You don't even want to fly your flag at half-mast when we sail out, and even the Burgomaster agreed to that! He's lowering the Town Hall flag."

"A loud mouth never gets you anywhere," Machiel's father said, his face calm. "And we did what we could. At least we managed to get the harbor in Colijn fixed up. And I won't fly my flag at half-mast. No one has died." An uneasy silence fell over them. Someone cleared his throat.

"Colijn of all places!" Skipper Domisse burst out. "Do *they* know what I'm supposed to do about school for Suzy and Anna? Or what my wife is supposed to do when I'm over there all day and have to sleep in one of those shacks?"

Only Moei Katrina saw how Skipper Domisse hastily wiped his eyes with his gnarled fingers. She took a step toward the ship, and her voice, usually so sharp, was soft:

"Now, Meindert . . . something will turn up. And your girls . . ." She hesitated and looked at Skipper Cevaal. "They'll stay with us," she finished briskly.

"Lord, Katrina, you're going to have to leave too," Skipper Domisse murmured, suddenly subdued. His fingers plucked at the net before him. Then he stood up very slowly. "All things come in threes—I've seen it happen before. First Arnemuiden and then Veere. That won't be the end of it."

They watched him go up the quay with sagging shoulders

and tired steps. Skipper Cevaal sighed. From the wharf Domisse called defiantly: "And I'll still fly my flag at half-mast. Tough for the movie man."

"It's all decided. Five of us can go along, that's all," Andries reported an hour later to the rest of the group.

"Well, that works out just right," Wolfert said excitedly. "Me and Andries and Joris and Machiel and . . ."

"No farmers allowed," Andries said firmly, but Wolfert refused to be put off. He had made up his mind to go along on this trip and have a part in The Plan, and Andries had lost a bit of his spirit. Only Machiel understood why. He also understood why Andries did not want to be on his father's ship, why he had moved heaven and earth to arrange that he would be on the *Tho 16,* Machiel on the *Ve 20,* and Tannie on a boat from Arnemuiden.

Wolfert set all his glibness to proving that since farmers had an interest in the Delta Plan, he belonged with the rest of the gang when the fleet sailed. Finally, even Andries was almost convinced, and Wolfert clinched the argument:

"After all, I was the one who thought up The Plan," he pointed out. "And I'll represent the Walcheren farmers."

"But what about me?" Tannie cried.

"No girls allowed," her brother decided, but now both Joris and Machiel protested, Joris because he couldn't stand to see Wolfert go and Tannie stay, and Machiel because it suddenly struck him that soon, when he was in Colijn, he would never see Tannie again. Well, maybe he would, but . . .

"If Wolfert comes, Tannie comes too," he said so positively the others gave in without a fight. Tannie smiled at Machiel, and he blushed crimson:

"All right, all right, that'll do."

"I'll do my very, very best," Tannie promised fervently.

"Just act natural," Andries said hastily. "It's easy as pie. You just go down into the fo'c's'le and get to the engine. Someone'll stand watch in the meantime. Then you just take . . . look— if this is the engine, you just turn . . ."

Two weeks later, while a farewell ceremony was being held in the Guild Hall, Andries saw his chance to rehearse The Plan. Everyone was inside listening to speeches about the closing of the harbor, and there was no one around to spy on them. He signaled the group to come along to the boats lying completely unattended in the harbor. On board the *Ve 20* the children crept into the forecastle. It was dark, and Tannie and Joris did not feel at ease. Even Wolfert found little to say, and Andries had to repeat his instructions three times before he could be sure everyone had understood.

"Have you got that now?" he asked urgently, looking into Machiel's face.

"Oh, come on!" Machiel said indignantly.

"Well, I meant the others." Andries snapped. "Come on, Tannie," he almost snarled. "At least repeat what I told you."

"You stand in front of the engine like this," Tannie repeated obediently, "and then you turn the little doohickey out —fump!—like that. You put it in your pocket, and there you are! You climb on deck again, looking as if butter wouldn't melt in your mouth! And if they ask where you were, you say you were looking for your friend." She took a deep breath and looked at Andries, blinking triumphantly.

"Well, okay. Could be worse," he admitted. "Couldn't be much easier, either. And when the boat doesn't start, you look completely innocent, hear?" He looked around threateningly, meeting Joris's steady look.

"Just leave it to me," Joris promised. He was much surer of himself these days. After all, a Plan like theirs was really something. It might even make the papers! In any case, it was a far cry from delivering shoes. And his father would have to see that he would not be able to shut his son up in the cobbler shop for the rest of his life; greater things lay in store for him.

"Maybe it will make the papers," he wished out loud.

"I'd rather it didn't," Tannie said thoughtfully.

Machiel carefully stuck his head out of the forecastle and pulled it back in again.

"Come on out now," he hissed. "I don't see them yet, but they might be here any minute."

The others hoisted themselves after him and blinked in the bright light.

"Just look at all those cars," Joris said, impressed.

"Real snazzy people!"

"They've invited everyone," Wolfert remarked. "Except for the people from the Waterworks Authority, because the Burgomaster says no one ever asked to have the dam here." Carefully he watched Machiel's reaction, but the boy was in no mood to be angry. He was thinking about The Plan, beginning to realize he would be working against his father. On the one hand he would be defending Veere; on the other hand, if it worked, The Plan would involve his father, too, and Machiel wasn't quite sure how he would take it.

An echoing voice resounded from the Guild Hall: ". . . earlier in our history, too, fishermen were driven out of this town. My friends, in eleven days the whole fleet will definitely . . ."

"Eleven days!" Tannie said restlessly. "What a long time!"

"Well, if you can't wait, just let us know," Andries said nastily. He looked at Machiel. "Maybe you and I should do it alone."

"No, no. All together. That's final," Machiel answered hastily. Without the others he would feel still more unsure of himself. And just imagine if he suddenly didn't dare carry out his part!

"Well, all right. Then I'll repeat the instructions for the last time," Andries said. "And you'd better get it right, or else! We'll take three ships, one from Arnemuiden, one from Tholen, and one from Veere. We can raise enough Cain with just those three if it works out right. Tannie and Wolfert will take the *Arn 14*. I'll handle the *Tho 16* with Joris. Skipper Bouterse said okay but no racket on board. And Machiel will go on the *Ve 20*. The moment I give the signal we all walk casually to our ships, like this—as if we weren't planning a thing. And when the music starts, the . . ."

A shattering fanfare burst from behind the wall, and the children jumped with fright. Andries gave an extra little jump just to show he had meant to jump in the first place.

"Listen, it's the Zeeland anthem," Machiel said when he had recovered. Behind the walls the shattering trumpets blared; the children felt the sound all the way down to their stomachs. Andries cleared his throat again and looked around the little circle. "Okay. Got it now?"

12
THE LAST SHIPS
THROUGH THE
VEERE GAP

As long as they lived the children would not forget the outcome of their Plan.

The fishing boats were ready early in the morning. Exchanging significant looks, the children felt like the heroes of an ancient tale. That morning there had been something mysterious about the little town they had lived in all their lives, something magical they had never felt before. It was as if they were seeing everything for the very first time.

"Pssst! There he comes!" Machiel said.

"Who?" Andries turned around.

"The producer, who else? Keep still. They're starting!"

"Let's go," Andries commanded, but he didn't feel at ease. Everything was so different today. When they passed his father's boat, it suddenly occurred to him that after this day the *Ve 13* would never sail from Veere again. Somehow, with all the talk he had never quite realized what the dam would mean to his father's ship.

"You take the top button," Tannie practiced softly. Machiel started out of his reverie.

"Did you say something?" he asked, more curtly than he meant to.

"N-n-n-no. N-n-n-nothing," Tannie stuttered. "I . . . I was just thinking."

"On board!" Andries announced, just as the fanfare stopped, the band resting for a few bars. Tourists stared at the Town Hall to which the invited guests would go. Never, not even during the summer, had there been so many strangers in Veere, and no one saw the children, four boys and a girl ducking into the forecastles.

The gray March weather hung above the ships; a droning helicopter whirled overhead. The sea gulls slowly smacked their tremendous wings together, and their cries rang above the upright masts.

In the engine room of the *Arn 14,* Tannie, almost choking with excitement, tried to do what Andries had explained to her. Wolfert hadn't dared. At the last minute he had said casually:

"I'd better keep watch on deck. If the skipper happens to come by I can keep him talking." He looked anxiously around. But Tannie suspected he didn't know what spark plugs were, or how to go about getting them out. Spark plugs: ". . . part of the engine generating an electric spark which ignites the fuel mixture in the cylinder . . ." she repeated feverishly in the darkness. She had looked up the word in the dictionary and learned the definition by heart. Of course it didn't help much if you didn't know what a fuel mixture was. She was hot and uncomfortable. Wouldn't it . . . would she be able . . With an effort she controlled herself.

"Let's go, Tannie. Don't be scared!" she ordered softly. She looked the engine over carefully, felt it, just as the boys had done on the *Ve 20*. The boys! They'd been so sure she wouldn't be able to do it. Well, they'd soon see! A little iron thing . . . yes, exactly . . . Suddenly she saw what she was looking for. With a quick movement of her hand she unscrewed it, put it in her pocket, peeped through the trap door and climbed, quick as a rabbit, up into the light, just as Wolfert stuck his head through the opening.

"Do you have it?" he asked, and when Tannie nodded he stared at her with undisguised admiration.

"Of course," she said. She tapped her pocket significantly. "Nothing to it."

"Hey! You're quite a kid!" Wolfert remarked. Tannie accepted the tribute graciously. It wasn't often her brother praised her.

"Easier than I thought," she confessed.

It was all over, and Wolfert silently gave thanks and sighed in relief.

"Look over there!" He pointed. "There's the *Ve 13*, Andries's father's ship, with its flag at half-mast."

The two children stood silently leaning over the railing of the *Arn 14*, watching the ships fill with skippers and important visitors. Shutters clicked and movie cameras whirred. The helicopter droned about overhead. There was so much noise they couldn't hear each other any more. The boat rocked softly on the splashing water, and now and then it bumped dully against the pier.

There were many important people on the *Tho 16*. It was late when the Burgomaster announced that this ship would carry the most important guest, perhaps even the Queen's deputy. Skipper Bouterse was on edge. He looked around restlessly for his mate and shouted at him to check the engine again, perhaps even give it a trial run. After all, you never knew. The man had come back immediately and told him that a spark plug was missing! The skipper, quite out of sorts with the unusual trip and the unexpected load of important visitors he had to carry, uttered only one terse word, then went straight down and replaced the missing spark plug with another he always kept in reserve.

Now he stood tight-lipped at the tiller. Sharply he scanned the crowds pressing against the railing. Who, of all the people there, had plotted that little surprise? His eyes lit on Andries Domisse and his friend, and the skipper's face softened for a moment. Clever kid, that Andries; helps out like an adult on his father's ship. He'll make one of the best skippers around. But what's to become of him? There aren't many opportunities left. Too bad his father is so hard to get along with these days. Not that I can't sympathize . . . But who the devil had taken . . . His eyes searched on, while Andries stood at the railing, cheerful and terribly pleased with himself.

"How did you ever dare!" Joris said in a muffled tone.

"Went fine, didn't it? After all, we agreed to do it." Andries tried to sound cool.

"Yes . . . yes," Joris stuttered. He would have liked to have done it himself, but Andries had decided he should stand watch. He had consoled himself with the thought that that was sabotaging too.

"What does the thing look like, exactly?" he asked curiously. Andries pulled the spark plug out of his pocket, carefully looking over his shoulder to make sure he wasn't being watched.

But everyone was busy with his own affairs: the fishermen seeing to their boats, the Burgomaster busy with his guest, the musicians with their playing, the tourists with their cameras and the little boys in the street simply screaming and yelling. In all the bustle of this day there was no one who paid any attention to them.

"Imagine, a little piece of steel like that . . ." Joris marveled.

"Well, it's important enough!" Andries said with a warning look. "Watch out. I'm going to throw it overboard. They'll never find it. One, two . . ."

With a little plop the *Tho 16*'s spark plug disappeared into the harbor of Veere. The boys looked at each other, Andries triumphant and Joris glowing; his heart swelled with delight because Andries was treating him like a fisherman today. Proudly he said:

"Whatever else happens, they won't make a monkey of the *Tho 16*!"

The *Ve 20* rocked slowly on the water. Machiel stood on the deck staring straight into the depths beneath him, his hands in his pockets. He had just been down in the engine room. Then he had come up again. There was his father, leaning on the wheel. He was alone. Skipper Cevaal had wanted no one on board today besides his sons, and he had refused to dip his flag to half-mast.

Andries stood on the deck of the *Tho 16*, Wolfert and Tannie on the *Arn 14*. Their heads disappeared and reappeared in the masses of people hurrying about. Machiel looked at Andries waving and pointing. Probably afraid I might forget, Machiel thought. Trying to reassure his friend, Machiel went back into the forecastle. He sighed. At any rate, they couldn't say it was a complicated job. He touched his fingers to the spark plug and pulled back again. He had never seen his father as he was today, his face so set, almost as if he weren't really there, almost as if his thoughts were years and years away.

Footsteps sounded on the deck, and on the quay the band struck up. Again Machiel stretched his fingers out. Now he'd do it.

But it was as though his hand would not do what they had all agreed upon, and Machiel felt resistance in himself to the whole Plan, which suddenly seemed pointless. Would The Plan really help his father? Would it mean anything at all to the fishermen? He would be making a fool of his father—Machiel was sure of that now. Again, down in the dark forecastle, he saw his father's face. Was he still standing on deck as before? Was he—was he perhaps thinking of Machiel's mother? She had seen him leave from this very quay the first time he had sailed out in the ship he had built with his own hands.

Machiel's fingers were still curled around the spark plug. You had to do what you promised; he had said he would go along with the others. Should he . . . But they were already convinced that he was on Allard's side.

Someone started down the stairs, darkening the trap door above the boy. His father's voice, controlled as always, floated down to him:

"Well, Machiel. That's a good idea, checking the engine. After all, you never can tell with a new engine like that. You're going to make a fine skipper, I know."

Machiel was silent for a second; then he turned around. They looked at each other for an instant in the gloom; in the shadows Machiel saw his father's eyes and realized how much he loved him.

"Yes," he said. "I was just checking it over. It's fine." His voice was normal, but he had pulled back his hand. The others would have to think what they pleased. From today on, nothing would be the same in Veere—not the harbor, not the people.

Hundreds of people were standing on the dikes and the wharves when the signal to leave was given at one o'clock. The twenty cutters steamed out, one after the other. They dipped over the water, slow and stately. Above the ships the helicopter whirled, darting nervously from one ship to the other. Ahead of the shrimp boats the orange lifeboat drew white stripes of foam through the water.

Machiel heard one of the cameramen shouting across the water: "Hold it there!" On board a black and green ship from Arnemuiden, three men in fishermen's garb bent busily over their work. But as soon as they saw the camera coming at them they dropped their arms to their sides like sticks and froze into their stiffest portrait faces.

"No, no! Don't look at us!" The producer's powerful voice rang over the water, and the men relaxed again at their work.

Andries would never forget the terrible moment when the deck of the *Tho 16* started to throb beneath his feet. His mouth fell open, and his eyes stared unbelievingly at Joris, who frowned gravely back. Hadn't Joris seen Andries take the spark plug and throw it overboard? Without a spark plug, no ship could move—Andries was quite sure of that. No one could tell him anything about ships' engines. Andries looked down at his feet, planted wide apart on the deck in his usual posture. The deck throbbed; the engine turned; the ship moved.

Andries swallowed hard, and his eyes sought out the *Arn 14.* A pair of heads stuck over the railing and disappeared below. A moment later, the *Arn 14,* too, solemnly left the pier. And there . . . there right behind the lifeboat . . . Andries ran his tongue over his bone dry lips: the *Ve 20* was moving too, with Machiel on deck as big as life. He leaned over the railing as if nothing at all had ever been planned. He stood next to his father, not even looking around. The two Cevaals looked so much alike that Andries cursed inwardly, furious that everything had gone wrong, jealous, too, of Machiel and his father, sailing off together so calmly. He knew the *Ve 20*'s departure was no accident or coincidence. Grimly he stared at the cutter and then turned his head again toward the *Arn 14*. Wolfert and Tannie waved their arms despairingly, and it was obvious that they were very disappointed.

"They're signaling to us," Joris called.

Andries groaned. In heaven's name, what had happened? Were they all bewitched? He ran about the ship, back and forth, left and right; he was underfoot everywhere and stepped on everyone's toes. But the exodus was in full swing. There were shouts and calls and the noise of the film cameras. With all the other ships, the *Tho 16* sailed in a mighty convoy through the Veere Gap.

"You did it wrong!" Wolfert hissed when they realized the ship was moving.

"I didn't! It isn't true!" Tannie cried, almost in tears. "It's still in my pocket—I'll show you! And I didn't want to . . . I only wanted to . . ." It was all too much, and poor Tannie burst into tears.

"Keep still," her brother said, poking her none too gently. "If they see you standing here and howling they'll think we're up to something. After all, nothing has happened yet . . ."

Tannie stopped crying, but then she thought of the others. Oh, what would they think of her!

"Girls!" Andries would say scornfully. And he would be right, at that. Anxiously she looked back at the quay.

"They're not there!" she shouted shrilly. Wolfert turned his head nervously and searched the convoy for the other ships. Then he saw the *Ve 20* with Machiel and his father standing at the wheel.

"There it is!" he cried. Now they weren't the only ones . . .

"And the *Tho 16* too!" Tannie pointed. Her wrist peeped out of her coat, and the tears dried on her cheeks. Wolfert crept a little closer to his sister. He felt he shouldn't have made her do the dirty work.

The entire trip the children brooded over the result of their ill-fated adventure; they did not see Veere disappearing into the distance until it looked like a little pen drawing, or the people on board the ships, or the ship with all the guests beneath the flag at half-mast. They hardly saw the fisherwomen with their skirts like sails, or the new dams they skimmed past while people waved from the shore. Shouts came to them from the sea walls, but they hardly noticed. Anxiously they rehearsed what they would say to each other when they reached Colijnsplaat.

They were there before they knew it.

In the midst of the ear-splitting racket that burst out, the uproar of officials shaking each others' hands and speaking solemn words, bands striking up with a roar, fishermen and tourists, reporters and photographers chattering busily and pushing their way through the crowds, the little group of children stood facing each other in heavy silence.

"I told you . . ." Andries said threateningly. He was so furious he didn't even raise his voice.

"You didn't even do it yourself," Machiel countered, seeming calm. Only Tannie noticed his hands opening and closing, opening and closing at his sides.

"Not because I didn't want to!" Andries screamed. "I went through with it! Joris here can prove it! But you—you just chickened out at the last minute. Can't you see, I can't trust you any more! Just because of your father . . ." He almost choked on his words.

"Yes, because of my father," Machiel said curtly. "And you can think what you like. I've had enough." He turned on his heel and walked away.

Behind him he heard Tannie crying, and he slowed his step for a moment. Now she'd get the worst of it. Suddenly, despite his anger, Machiel had to laugh, just for an instant. Tannie had not removed a spark plug but a fuse from the generator for the spotlights. She was even showing it around proudly to prove it hadn't been her fault. Andries grabbed it furiously out of her hand and threw it as far as he could.

"I honestly . . . honestly . . . I did . . ." Tannie bawled, and even Wolfert said something soothing, but it was too late. He had already let his sister take the rap.

Machiel turned around brusquely. "Come along," he said, drawing Tannie away by the arm, and before the others could say anything, a band pushed through the group like a flying wedge.

"Come along, we'll have a Coke," Machiel said.

And they left, Tannie still sobbing, Machiel resentful and yet relieved at what he had done; he had chosen between the gang and his father.

He knew now that he would probably not become a fisherman, but that had nothing to do with it, he assured himself. That was another matter.

13
COLIJNSPLAAT

"He was furious, you know! And he accused me!" Tannie's voice was still shaky. "And he said nothing had helped—that's what he said too. And he said he should have known it all along because . . ."

Machiel and Tannie sat talking in a cafe near the harbor in Colijn. A waiter approached them and asked, "Well, sir and madam, what'll it be?"

Openmouthed, Tannie stared at the waiter, but Machiel nudged her softly under the table. As though he did it every day, he said: "Two Cokes, please." Tannie turned toward Machiel, completely staggered. She forgot what she wanted to tell him, and admiration shone out of her eyes. Indifferently, Machiel slouched in his chair as he saw people around him do. The cafe was jammed; words buzzed and droned like bees around them, and no one even looked at the children at their table by the window.

The boy in the white jacket brought the tray with two bottles and two glasses, balancing it on his upraised hand:

"There you are, sir!" Something in his voice made Tannie blush, but Machiel looked up without a word and nodded briefly. The boy disappeared. Tannie had followed the whole thing in amazement. What a look Machiel had! Just like his father! No one would ever put anything over on him.

"Do you . . . do you have enough money for—for all this?" she asked in confusion.

"What do you think!" Machiel answered, rummaging in his trouser pockets. "I got a whole guilder from my father because —well because today's special. Do you want some gingerbread too?"

"Oh, no!" Tannie almost choked. "You mustn't throw away your money like that!"

"I'm being careful!" Machiel answered.

"Oh, well," Tannie said, a bit embarrassed. She took little sips of her Coke and looked at Machiel over the rim of her glass. It was funny to be sitting here. Nice, too. But suddenly she remembered everything the others had said before Machiel had rescued her.

"Andries said it was all your fault . . ."

Machiel set his glass down with such a bang that some of the Coke spilled.

"*My* fault! Oh, that's too much!"

"Because you wanted me to come along." Tannie pushed her drink back and forth, but she kept an eye on Machiel's face. It was dark and frowning now as it had been that day when they saw the caissons and had the quarrel afterward.

"Gets better and better," Machiel remarked sarcastically.

He paused and then said more calmly, "Well, there's so much going on today. We'll talk about it another time." He pretended he didn't really care, but Tannie saw that he did.

"Of course it was pretty silly of me," she admitted, "taking the wrong spark plug. It was . . . it was . . ." she looked at Machiel shamefacedly.

"A fuse," he said, without expression.

"How do you know?" Tannie cried.

Machiel shrugged. He bit his lip to keep from laughing, but Tannie was drawing lines in the little lake of Coca-Cola he had spilled. She didn't look up.

"The thing was right where Andries said . . . loose, you know. You could just pull it out like that. Well, and then the ship went off after all . . ."

"Of course," Machiel remarked.

"Wolfert's a windbag!" Tannie exclaimed. "*He* didn't dare. And he scolded me hardest of all. It's always like that!" And Tannie began to cry all over again.

"Oh, well," Machiel said. "You know how he is."

"Yes," Tannie said, sobbing. "But it's . . . it's . . ." and fresh tears rolled down her cheeks as Machiel watched her anxiously.

"Tannie . . ."

She looked up at him in embarrassment. Neither of them knew what to say, but Tannie pulled herself together first. She finished her Coke and put the glass back on the table. Then, in one gesture, she wiped her eyes and mouth with her handkerchief. Machiel pretended to be staring out the window with great interest.

"It's just that they're always down on you these days," Tannie said softly when she had blown her nose. "And on me because I'm a girl."

Machiel didn't know what to answer. Thoughtfully he stared at his glass.

"And you . . . They're going to start ignoring us both pretty soon," Tannie continued. "Just like . . ."

"Like the boy from the Waterworks Authority?" Machiel asked without looking up.

Tannie nodded. "But what difference does it make?" she said. "All that fuss with Andries about The Plan. We should have known before it wouldn't help at all. At least it wouldn't help your father. He would have to leave anyway. And tomorrow at school they'll all be in a foul mood. You'll see."

"What's the difference?" Machiel said stiffly. "I'm leaving anyway."

"Yes, *you* are . . ." she sounded spiteful. "But I'll be alone with that bunch in Veere. Where's the fun in that? And then that fuss about the new boy!"

Tannie looked at Machiel directly now. "I've been going around with Allard's sister a bit."

Machiel looked up in surprise. "You?"

"Yes, me," Tannie said.

"But she's only in the fourth grade!"

"I know. But she was just as lost as her brother. So I took her home with me a couple of times. Children like that always find something to do on a farm. Her name's Celestine. Nice name, isn't it? She sings well too—sang me a song."

Behind them, glasses rattled and chatter swept the little room. In the harbor at least fifty masts bobbed up and down. Machiel leaned his chin on his hands and watched Tannie. She didn't lower her eyes but looked at him trustingly.

"I go over there quite often," Machiel told her. "It's much more fun than you might think. Allard knows a lot about how they build dams and things like that."

Tannie said nothing, but she listened carefully, and Machiel found himself telling her all about the new boy, and how from the very first he had found Allard fascinating. After all, he was connected with the things that Machiel had been curious and concerned about from the day the dam was begun. His thoughts had been in a turmoil, turning over and over in his head for months. Sometimes he would think of going to fishing school and to sea, other times he would choose Junior High as his teacher advised. If he went to high school, he would study for a completely different career. His confusion showed, especially today. He had wanted to go along with The Plan and might have found it easy on another ship, but not on his father's.

"You haven't told your father and Dingenis you'd rather not be a fisherman, have you?" Tannie asked.

"That's just it," Machiel said. "If you knew him . . . And Dingenis. He hates those people with the Authority. I'd just better keep out of his way with that idea!"

He sat silently at the bare wooden table. The sound of the sea came from outside—you could hear it as clearly here as in Veere.

"Let's go to the quay and see if the bus is ready," Tannie suggested.

"No. First tell me what you think of this." Machiel's voice sounded so definite that Tannie had to listen.

"I'll tell you something," Machiel said. "I really . . . I really want to be what Allard's father is—an engineer. But I don't dare say so!" He didn't look at Tannie, but she saw his fingers twining nervously in and out of one another. She thought about it carefully. If Machiel carried out his plan he wouldn't have an easy time at home, not with his family. Everyone would have something to say about it, not only his father and Dingenis, but his Uncle Meindert and Moei Katrina too.

"Couldn't you just tell your father alone?" she asked. "He's not the worst of them—I mean, he looks as if he would understand . . ." She was almost frightened at her own courage and just a bit embarrassed.

"That's true," Machiel agreed.

"Well, then," Tannie said cheerfully. "It'll work out all right. My mother always says, 'One must never do anything that goes against the grain.'"

"Against my grain," Machiel said slowly. "I don't really hate fishing. But I prefer the other. I don't know why—but building something like that . . . Anyway, it still has something to do with the sea—with—well—with safety, you know. But I don't think I'll tell them yet. I'll wait a while. Maybe . . . Tannie!" he burst out suddenly. "I want to see the closing of the dam so badly!"

"Yes." Tannie thought it over. "The Veere people aren't going, are they? Mrs. Hubregse said the other day, 'Do they expect us to dig our own graves?' How silly. There isn't anything being dug!"

"Well," Machiel answered. "They're right in a way after all. But I want to see it because of the construction itself, you know—how the caissons are placed in the gap. They set them together accurately to the inch. Do you know the *Asia* and the *Europa* are coming?"

Tannie merely nodded, though she didn't know what they were. It was much more important to her that the Queen would probably be there.

"Is anyone in your house going?" she asked.

"No. They're hardly going to be in Veere any more. My father will only be home on Sunday."

"Yes . . ." In her mind's eye, Tannie saw the uncomfortable green barracks the fishermen would live in for the time being, and the empty places in the Veere homes.

"Say, couldn't we go together? It'll be a kind of—almost a kind of farewell, won't it? Because you'll be leaving soon after that."

Machiel looked at her thoughtfully. "Maybe," he said.

"They're all angry at us anyway," Tannie continued persuasively. "Wolfert even said . . . he said . . ."

"Well, what?"

"That you haven't really been part of the group for a long time. That you just pretended to go along with us, but you always hung around those caissons."

"Oh, now really!" Machiel cried. He knew that Wolfert was untrustworthy, changeable as the weather. But this . . .

"Don't take it to heart," Tannie said. "I'll get even with him!"

"Forget it," Machiel stopped her. "I'll take care of it myself. Besides, what do I care?" He was silent, but suddenly he continued: "If he's told that to Andries . . ."

"Maybe Andries wouldn't believe him," Tannie said hopefully, but Machiel only sniffed. In the last few weeks it had been quite clear what Andries thought of him.

"What do I care anyway?" he said. "It's just that . . ."

He's thinking that he'll have to go to school with Andries in Colijnsplaat, Tannie realized. Aloud she said:

"They gave me a hard time, you know." Across the table Machiel just barely touched her hand; then he stood up.

"Tell me, when the dam's completed . . . ." he began.

"Yes . . ."

"You can get from Veere to Colijnsplaat pretty easily by bike. I mean . . ."

"Yes!"

The two of them left the table, and Machiel paid the cashier. He waited at the door for Tannie to go through first. She blushed; everything was so different today.

For the last time that day Machiel looked at the ships lying calmly row after row in their new harbor. Their masts stuck straight up against the gray sky, just as they had at home. There would be no shrimp boats in Veere any more, nor any fish carts rattling across the quay. For a sudden moment Machiel felt the way he did when his father had told him about his mother, that day of the great flood.

"Well, that's it," he said to Tannie as they walked to the bus stop across the unfamiliar quay.

From that day on the members of the gang began to drift apart. Mr. Risseeuw noticed that the feverish whispering he had had to forbid so often during class had stopped. He saw that Machiel and Allard now openly sought each other out and sometimes went home from school together, and that Andries wandered off to the quay alone. Skipper Cevaal noticed too, but not because Machiel had said anything yet of his decision not to go to fishing school in September; he was still afraid to talk about it with his father. Every Saturday evening as Machiel was about to say something he saw his father's set face, and his throat closed. He didn't want to spoil the weekend, and he tried to talk about something else. But Skipper Cevaal remarked:

"I never see you with Andries any more. Had a fight or something?"

"What do you mean?" Machiel asked defensively. "Did his father say something?"

"No, I just thought you were always together, and you wanted to go to fishing school together soon."

"Oh, that . . ." Machiel's hand opened and shut mechanically. Now he could say it. Fishing school . . . Had he really wanted that so much? It seemed impossible.

"Actually, I'd like . . . I want . . ." he began. He looked down, and his father couldn't hear him clearly.

"The two of you will have to come along on board again some night," Skipper Cevaal said cheerfully. "Seems there's going to be a teacher's meeting in Middleburg. You would be able to get back to Veere from Colijn, wouldn't you? How about it?"

Machiel hesitated, and he knew his father was watching him.

"Maybe Andries ought to go with his own father," Machiel remarked. "That way we would be able to take someone else along, like the new fellow from the Waterworks. He doesn't know anything about fishing . . ." At least he had made a start. But he sensed his father's cool gaze above his head, as cool as his voice, which only said, "Well, we'll see."

"Well, we'll see." Machiel answered in the same words a couple of days later when Tannie started asking again about their plan to go and watch the closing of the dam.

"We'll keep it a secret," Tannie decided. "Or Wolfert will butt in again. And he mustn't come along!" Machiel muttered absently:

"Yes, yes, that'll be fine." He was thinking about how they would get a good spot. Anyone could go to the dike in Vrouwen polder. But to be able to see everything close up . . .

Tannie seemed to guess his thoughts. "Of course there'll be all sorts of gentlemen in black suits swarming about again, and guests and people from the Waterworks Authority. We'll never even get close!"

"That's it!" Machiel cried suddenly. "The Waterworks Authority, of course. I'll ask Allard if he knows of anything." And off he went.

Allard wasn't at home when Machiel arrived, and his mother didn't know where he had gone. "He may be wandering around the caissons," she suggested softly. Her dark eyes looked carefully at the fishing boy, but Machiel muttered a shy goodby and turned away. A little disappointed, he walked slowly over the bridge again and up the long quay.

Suddenly he heard Allard's voice shouting, "Machiel! Hi! Want a ride?"

"Sure," Machiel answered, settling himself on the back of the bicycle. "I just went to your house, but your mother didn't know where you were. I wanted to ask you . . . Allard, it's a secret, but Tannie and I want to go see the closing of the dam by ourselves, not with the others. Could you get us a place close up?"

Allard hesitated. "Gee, I wish I could, but . . ."

"Forget it, it's all right," Machiel assured him. "I just thought I'd ask."

They rode on silently, Allard pedaling hard against the strong wind. "Say," Machiel asked, "are you going to be an engineer, too?"

Allard whistled scornfully.

"Not me! Who wants to be cold-shouldered everywhere and send your children to different schools over and over again? And have them pestered all the time? And work day and night and never come home? And have to listen to your children . . . No, that's not for me. I'm going to be . . ." But Allard had stopped to catch his breath. Then he went on, a bit less intensely: "For you it's different, of course."

"I don't see why," Machiel said stiffly.

"Your mother drowned here." Allard's right arm made such a wide sweep that the bicycle teetered sharply. Machiel held on to Allard's jacket, but he listened carefully.

"If that had happened to me . . ."

"Well, what?" Machiel asked.

There was an advantage to carrying on a conversation on a bicycle, Machiel realized. You didn't have to look at the other person.

"Then I'd do everything in my power to fight that water. That makes sense, after all!" Allard screamed with the last of his breath. "I'm going to be a teacher. You're home nice and snug every evening!"

They bounced along the cobblestones of the Square, and Machiel jumped off. Allard whipped the bicycle around. "So long," he called. His face was red with exertion, but he smiled happily.

"Hey! Thanks for the ride," Machiel yelled back as he stretched his legs.

14
THE DAM IS CLOSED

THE children sat on the wall beneath the Campveerse Tower, just as before. But they were not gazing at the incoming fishing boats as they had in the past; they were looking at the six caissons looming before them like a wall. A single breech barely let the sea through.

"My father says they only pretended they couldn't manage it, so they could get more people to come and watch them," Wolfert said.

Allard van Beusekom's only answer was to screw his eyes almost shut against the bitter east wind and rain. But he was watching the tremendous outlines of the six concrete structures.

"Anyway, there they are," Tannie said.

A few days ago the first caisson had been dragged out toward the Gap. There it was fastened with heavy lines to one of the corners of the Walcheren dam head so it could be turned inward like a gate. A couple of days later the second caisson lay in the breakers like a rock. On Thursday, the third one had been set in place. Then the fourth, and the fifth. When the sixth caisson was being moved into position, Joris had asked: "Why do they trail it around like that in the sea before they set it down?"

"So they can maneuver it against the current," Allard answered quietly. He noticed the others were listening too. Slowly, very slowly they were beginning to accept him. And since the caisson maneuvers had started they had begun asking him all sorts of questions. Allard sighed. Too bad getting to know people always took such a long time. The Gap was almost closed now. How long would his father still be working here?

Now Tannie mused, "It's like moving a bunch of factories. The royal yacht, the *Piet Hein,* is coming too!"

"So are we, aren't we, Machiel?" Andries asked.

"Who knows," Machiel answered vaguely.

"Oh, stop daydreaming all the time!" Andries scolded.

"Wouldn't do you any harm to do a bit of that," Tannie remarked snippily. Anxiously she looked at Machiel. If he was thinking about *their* plan she'd better change the subject.

But Andries was busy thinking about what Mr. Risseeuw had told them this morning. The whole class was to go this afternoon and watch the closing of the dam. They were to stand on the dike at the side of the dam and sing with the other schools when the seventh caisson was set in place.

"That should be really something, shouldn't it?" Andries said. "We'll be waving our little flags about while they fill in the gap. And then we'll sing the national anthem." His voice made it sound like a great joke, but in his eyes Machiel read a final desperate appeal—to him, who had always been Andries's closest friend, to Machiel, with whom he had sailed on the *Ve 20.* For a moment all the trouble, the suspicions, the growing uncertainty, between them were gone.

Machiel saw that Tannie was watching his face as anxiously as Andries. What should he answer? Did he have to tell them what he was planning himself? That weeks before he had decided to go with Tannie? They wouldn't understand. They'd say he was betraying them. And he couldn't explain it very well either. He had not even been able to talk to his father yet, and so he said impatiently: "I'll go along with whatever you say. But it's not that easy—we ought to know that by now."

Andries dropped his hand and drew his eyebrows together in a frown. "The least you could do is go along with us in deciding not to stand by and watch. And sing, too!" he said gruffly.

"He'll promise that all right, won't you, Machiel?" said Tannie in her sweetest voice.

"Oh, come off it!" Machiel snapped at her. "If anyone doesn't want to sing, well, he won't sing. That's all."

At that moment the school bell rang through the town.

When class was over that day Andries said in a loud voice: "Okay. It's all set, then!"

But secretly Machiel assured Tannie: "Yes, we're going—*before* the bus leaves from school. But you'd better figure on getting into trouble with the rest of them."

"I don't care!" Tannie declared. "Besides, they won't even notice. And if they do, we'll be standing high and dry on the dike by then."

But if their friends didn't notice them leaving Veere secretly, Machiel's aunt certainly did. She was busily scrubbing the blue and white stoop while Mrs. Hubregse held the pail for her. Suddenly Machiel bounded through the open door.

"Watch out!" Moei Katrina shouted crossly. Angrily her eyes went to his face, and in one glance she saw his coat and his father's old binoculars under his arm.

"Your good coat!" she cried. "And where are you going, if I may ask?" She still held the brush between her rough hands, waiting for an answer. Mrs. Hubregse stood half bent, her bucket raised. Expectantly the two old women looked at the boy.

"I'm going out," Machiel informed them curtly, and obstinately closed his mouth.

His aunt looked at the binoculars again. Slowly she said: "You're going to the closing, of course."

"Suppose I am?" his voice was controlled, and he knew it.

"And do your father and Dingenis know about this?" she asked.

"No," Machiel said unexpectedly. "And I'm not planning to let everyone in on what I . . ." Suddenly Machiel was so furious at the woman's meddling that he screamed: "I have to sing the national anthem!"

Machiel's aunt stepped back in shock, dropped her brush and knocked the bucket over. The icy water streamed across Machiel's legs and he shot into the air.

"And now will you let me go or not! I can't stand it any more!" he yelled.

All at once Skipper Cevaal appeared and asked sternly, "What's going on here?"

Immediately Machiel stopped yelling at his aunt. His father looked sharply at the boy's flushed face, but Machiel avoided the glance. He was angry and obstinate, and his father realized that something more than the fuss with his aunt had disturbed him so much.

"Machiel," he said softly.

The tone of his father's voice was enough to make the resentment and suspicion disappear from Machiel's face.

"Come and walk with me," his father suggested. Slowly he led the boy across the Square and to the quay. They stopped where the *Ve 20* had always moored, and automatically rested their feet on their own ship's white bollard.

"You were going to the closing?"

Machiel nodded silently, and his father gazed ahead at the little gap left by the six caissons. There wasn't much of a horizon left.

"I want to see how it's done," Machiel said obstinately. "But those women always have something to say. They're always interfering."

"It's not that," Skipper Cevaal said. "It's just that they're at their wit's ends with all that's happening. And as a matter of fact . . ." He suddenly turned to face his son.

"Machiel, we don't talk much. But you mustn't think I haven't noticed you're worried about something. Tell me, you'd rather not be a fisherman any more, isn't that it? You want to be what the people with the Waterworks are. Am I right?"

Machiel didn't move; he hardly dared breathe. Had his father really known all along?

"I . . . uh . . . I never said . . ." he mumbled.

"You didn't have to. Even if I'm not home much . . . Well, I knew."

Quickly Machiel looked up. Was his father's voice suddenly different now? But the face next to him had not changed.

"I noticed you were only interested in the new dam, and the

caissons and everything they were building in the harbor. And I must say, it *is* an impressive thing. I've thought that myself these past few months. If you want to go there today I won't be angry, even though your uncle and I will not go, nor will the others. Go ahead, Machiel. Your mother . . ." Abruptly he stopped. After a moment he went on: "It's silly to belittle work like this, but we're the victims. I am not being childish, son, but today is a difficult day for us."

Again Machiel looked up. How many wrinkles and lines there were in his father's face! Suddenly Machiel thought how much his father had gone through alone. There was so much that he had neither wanted nor been able to talk to anyone about: Machiel's mother, and Veere, and the fishing and the dam. He had never complained, not about his own solitude, nor having to leave his birthplace, and now he would not hold his son back. Machiel cried out:

"Father, I *do*! I do still want to go to fishing school. I still can. I haven't said anything yet—not even to the teacher. And if you want . . . Then you won't . . ."

"Then you won't be so alone," he had meant to say. But he held it in. His father certainly wouldn't accept that.

"And I don't have to go to the closing either!" he decided generously.

But the skipper shook his head firmly. He even smiled, a bit wistfully.

"I wouldn't like it if you were going there out of sheer curiosity—like the people over there." His hand indicated the crowds on Fort The Hague Road, and boats near the Veere Gap.

"But since you have thought it over carefully, go ahead. I don't mind. Really."

Machiel hesitated. He was glad he could go, but something still held him back. He looked up again.

"Father, I thought . . . It isn't that I don't want to go to sea," he said. "You know that. It was just . . ."

Skipper Cevaal laughed. "How old are you, Machiel?" he asked.

"Twelve," Machiel answered promptly.

"Yes, twelve. When I was your age . . . I still remember. Twelve years old. At that age you think one thing today, another tomorrow. If you change your mind and want to go to sea later on, then we can still see about it. But a good education can't hurt anyone. If you get to be an engineer, figure out something like a sluice gate for us in East Schelde. Otherwise eventually we'll have to leave there too. And now get going before you-know-who catches you!"

Machiel turned, but his father caught him by the sleeve again:

"What was that Moei Katrina was saying? You have to sing at the dam closing? I've never heard you sing a single note!"

"And I can't!" Machiel said. A broad grin spread over his entire face, but the grin included more than the answer he had just given. He felt as if a great load had fallen from his shoulders.

"Well, are you going?" his father asked. And just then a long, high yell came around the corner of the quay: "Machieeeeel!"

It was Tannie. She was red and out of breath, and there was a huge rip in her blouse.

"Where *were* you?" she sobbed. "Your aunt said . . . And Wolfert . . . Just *look* at me!"

"You didn't say anything, did you?" Machiel asked her.

"Of course not," Tannie replied indignantly. "But he finds out everything. He tried to hold me back, and I got loose. And now look! My best blouse!" She bit her lip to keep back the tears, and then she saw Machiel's father. She turned red with fright and embarrassment.

"I . . . it was a new blouse!"

"Never mind. No one will see it!" Machiel said, feeling elated, and before Tannie could get upset all over again he grabbed her by the hand.

"There's the musselman with his cart. Hurry—we'll get a ride!"

They ran off, Machiel brighter and happier than he had ever been.

"Machiel, it's moving!" Tannie whispered, not knowing herself why she didn't dare say it out loud. Machiel didn't answer. Breathless and tense, he stared at the tremendous gray caisson which until now had lain still in the glittering water.

High above, the great flag of the Netherlands flew; you could see it waving back and forth.

"We made it after all!" Tannie sighed. Machiel nodded without taking his eyes off the stately, moving caisson. He was relaxed and happy because of his talk with his father. But at the moment he was especially happy because he and Tannie had had such good luck. An English television photographer had lost his assistant in the crowd and asked the two children to help him carry some of his equipment. Machiel and Tannie had acted as his escorts, each carrying a box. The three of them climbed to the very top of the dune where they had the best possible view.

And now the sea lay before them. The seventh caisson passed

right before their eyes. Machiel grasped the railing until his knuckles blanched so no one would notice how excited he was. Next to him Tannie kept her fists pressed hard against her cheeks.

Far behind Machiel and Tannie, an ant hill of adults and children teemed. All the schoolchildren from the villages around the Veere Gap were there.

"What are they going to do about the national anthem?" Tannie whispered. Machiel shrugged, grinning. Tannie looked around again. People were standing all along the dike—thousands of people.

Now and then the tugboat whistles blew short, clipped signals. The people watched with bated breath; adults and children stood staring in fascination. Without a sound, the seventh caisson approached the gap in the dam.

"Are we all here?" Mr. Risseeuw asked. He was on edge; it wasn't only the dam, everything was peculiar today. As the seventh caisson moved steadily to its place, Mr. Risseeuw was so busy counting the children that he didn't even notice it. Allard van Beusekom wasn't there. Well, the teacher thought, he's probably found a good place with the Waterworks people. "But wait! Where are Machiel and Tannie?" he suddenly asked. He scanned the rows again, and the children exchanged significant looks. They had long since noticed that the two were missing, and it had not improved their mood. They were beginning to get bored just standing on the dikehead, and Wolfert answered readily: "They left at least an hour before us."

Frowning, the teacher looked at Wolfert. But as Mr. Risseeuw asked him something, a shrill steam whistle shrieked and his words were lost. Then the teacher looked at his watch, then at Veere, shading his eyes. That white dot in the distance, could that be the *Piet Hein*? How long it was all taking! How would he be able to keep the children quiet? Brusquely Mr. Risseeuw whirled about as Wolfert suddenly shouted, pointing into the distance.

"There, sir!" he exclaimed.

"What is it?" Mr. Risseeuw demanded. "Is it the *Piet Hein*? But I just saw it myself . . ."

"No, sir. Tannie! And Machiel! Over on that little box, right ahead of the caisson. With the special guests!"

The teacher stared in astonishment at the two television trucks in front of the caisson, and the two children on their box.

"Quiet, there!" someone shouted from the dike, but Wolfert didn't care. Excitedly he told Mr. Risseeuw that Tannie had left an hour early. And Machiel . . .

"Oh, go back to your place!" the teacher cried suddenly, in a fury. At the same moment he decided that Tannie and Machiel would have to be punished somehow, but later, not in the midst of all this confusion and excitement.

Straining tensely, everyone watched the seventh caisson being moved inch by inch into the gap. Tugs ahead of it, tugs behind it, short warning signal blasts and tugboat captains shouting curt orders across the water through megaphones. Slowly the huge structure of concrete and steel began to turn as it was placed in the gap.

"Just look at those two standing over there, with a front row spot like that," Andries muttered. The other children, long since tired from standing around, agreed wholeheartedly with him. They forgot that they themselves had wanted to stand and watch from good spots.

"Quitters," Andries muttered in an angry tone.

Suddenly Mr. Risseeuw called out, "It's starting! Places, everyone!"

"It's taking a long time," a little boy near Machiel said to his father.

"Now watch this, Tannie!" Machiel exclaimed. "Here, you can see better if you stand on tiptoe. Now it's turning in the gap on its hinges. And then . . ."

Five tugboats pushed, pulled and pressed themselves with all their might against the walls of the gigantic caisson. Just a couple of inches more. The men on the corners of the caisson waited anxiously, ready to catch hold and make fast. Close by, the royal yacht, gleaming white, bobbed in the water, moored to a blue buoy. Helicopters with photographers whirred overhead. Thousands of people stood erect and waited tensely.

Only seconds to go . . .

And then the historic closing of the Veere Gap was completed, slowly and majestically.

An overwhelming racket of ships' whistles broke forth. The sound of rejoicing shrieked from the ships and across the water. The seventh caisson lay in its spot where moments before there had been a gap in the dam.

Mr. Risseeuw looked from the water to his class and from his class to the *Piet Hein*. The Queen was standing on the deck, surrounded by many people. The teacher raised his baton, let it fall again, and suddenly the Veere band burst into a fanfare. While the trumpets blared and the drums rattled out the beat, the singing of almost three hundred children sounded high and thin over the dike. The children forgot that they hadn't wanted to sing. Half of them sang too low, and the other half sang too high, but they didn't notice Mr. Risseeuw's anguished face. They were all looking at the Queen.

Seven immense caissons lay quietly under the broad Zeeland sky, and thousands of people swarmed around them: people on boats, barges and dinghies, on the dike and on the headland.

Fishermen from Veere and Arnemuiden watched with set faces, and one of them shook his head slowly at a newscaster who held out a microphone to him.

The royal yacht came closer over the water. High above the bridge of caissons, three burgomasters appeared. They shook hands, waved their hats and bowed before the Queen. Their coattails fluttered in the wind.

And the people from the Waterworks Authority stood to one side, fulfillment in their faces and guarded triumph in their eyes. They were still in their watertight boots and shirt sleeves. Machiel could see Mr. van Beusekom lay his hand on his son's shoulder.

Slowly, Machiel took Tannie by the arm and said, "My father knows. We had a talk and it's all right now."

The Netherlands national anthem blared. The dam was closed.